FROM THE
NANCY DREW FILES

THE CASE: The disappearance of boat designer Nick
   Lazlo leads Nancy into an investigation of murder.

CONTACT: Parker Wright's cousin Andy ran the boat
   building company with Nick.

SUSPECTS: Stan Yadlowski—a private detective
   hired to investigate Lazlo Designs' insurance
   claims. What was he really looking for when he
   broke into Nick's office?

   Annabel Lazlo—Nick's wife wants a divorce but
   doesn't want to lose her investment in the company
   . . . did she kill two birds with one bullet?

   Andy Devereux—Seeing that Nick stood in the
   way of his getting to know Annabel better, did he
   find a way to dissolve the partnership . . . for good?

COMPLICATIONS: Bullet holes . . . bloodstains . . .
   but no body! How can Nancy find a murderer
   when she can't even locate the victim?

Books in The Nancy Drew Files® Series

Available from ARCHWAY Paperbacks

The Nancy Drew Files ™

Case 81
Making Waves
Carolyn Keene

An Archway paperback edition is soon to be published. For information address ... Simon & Schuster ... For information address Pocket Books, 1230 Avenue of the Americas, New York, NY 10020

AN ARCHWAY PAPERBACK
Published by POCKET BOOKS
New York   London   Toronto   Sydney   Tokyo   Singapore

The sale of this book without its cover is unauthorized. If you purchased this book without a cover, you should be aware that it was reported to the publisher as "unsold and destroyed." Neither the author nor the publisher has received payment for the sale of this "stripped book."

This book is a work of fiction. Names, characters, places, and incidents are either the product of the author's imagination or are used fictitiously. Any resemblance to actual events or locales or persons, living or dead, is entirely coincidental.

AN ARCHWAY PAPERBACK *Original*

An Archway Paperback published by
POCKET BOOKS, a division of Simon & Schuster Inc.
1230 Avenue of the Americas, New York, NY 10020

Copyright © 1993 by Simon & Schuster Inc.
Produced by Mega-Books of New York, Inc.

All rights reserved, including the right to reproduce this book or portions thereof in any form whatsoever. For information address Pocket Books, 1230 Avenue of the Americas, New York, NY 10020

ISBN: 0-671-73085-1

First Archway Paperback printing March 1993

10 9 8 7 6 5 4 3 2 1

NANCY DREW, AN ARCHWAY PAPERBACK and colophon are registered trademarks of Simon & Schuster Inc.

THE NANCY DREW FILES is a trademark of Simon & Schuster Inc.

Cover art by Tricia Zimic

Printed in the U.S.A.

IL 6+

Making Waves

MAKING WAVES

Chapter

One

Wow! A cruise on a sailboat," Bess Marvin said to her friend Nancy Drew. "That's my idea of a perfect spring vacation!" She spoke loudly to be heard above the wind and tried to keep her blond hair from flying everywhere by holding it in a ponytail with one hand.

The two girls were in the backseat of a white Cadillac convertible with the top down. In front, Bess's new boyfriend, Parker Wright, and Nancy's longtime boyfriend, Ned Nickerson, were talking to Parker's cousin Andy Devereux, who was driving.

Andy and his parents had invited Parker, Bess, Nancy, and Ned to stay with them in Annapolis, Maryland, over the boys' spring break from Emerson College. As the Cadillac sped down the

Baltimore–Washington Highway on the way from the airport, Nancy couldn't help feeling excited. Not only were they on vacation, but they were going to help Andy sail his new boat, the *Skipper's Surprise,* in an upcoming regatta, the first sailboat race of the Annapolis Spring Series.

"It's not exactly a cruise, Bess," Nancy said. The wind had whipped Nancy's reddish gold hair into tangles, but the salty air felt invigorating. "If we're going to help crew Andy's boat for the race, that means 'trimming the mainsail' and 'grinding the jib.'"

Bess made a face. "You can trim and grind all you want. I'm going to put on my new bikini and get a tan."

Nancy laughed. She knew Bess had spent days picking out the perfect bathing suit, even though Nancy had warned her that Maryland spring weather would be too chilly for sunbathing.

"When we race, I'll mainly need you guys for ballast," Andy called over his shoulder. In his midtwenties, Andy had the same reddish hair and athletic build as his cousin Parker.

"Ballast?" Bess repeated, arching an eyebrow. "Is that something I can do while I'm sunbathing?"

Parker grinned and turned around to look at Bess. "Ballast is something heavy to help steady the boat and keep it balanced," he explained.

Bess tapped him on the shoulder, a look of

mock anger in her blue eyes. "Parker! Are you calling me heavy?"

"No way! You're perfect, Bess Marvin, and you know it." Parker's green eyes twinkled as he ran a hand through his thick hair. He and Bess had been dating only a short while, but Nancy could tell they really liked each other.

"Nancy and I both have some sailing experience," Ned reassured Andy. The wind had ruffled his brown hair into waves. Nancy was glad the two of them were finally getting to spend some time together. Her last case had been grueling for all four of them—Parker had been falsely accused of murdering a teaching assistant at Emerson College in a case Nancy called *Power of Suggestion.* Nancy was glad for the chance to really relax now.

Andy nodded. "Good. Nick Lazlo, my partner, is the skipper of the *Skipper's Surprise.* He'll be happy to have experienced sailors to crew. After a while, family and friends get sick of racing."

"You and Nick have a sailboat-building business, right?" Nancy asked, leaning forward in the back seat. Parker had told them a little about Andy's business during the flight to Maryland from the Midwest.

"Right. It's called Lazlo Designs," Andy replied. "Nick's the designer. I handle the sales and business end. Nick's got some great ideas that we're trying out on the *Skipper's Surprise.* In fact, the *Surprise* is our prototype for a new line of boats we're calling the Nican Forty. If she performs as well as we hope in Sunday's race, we'll start manufacturing the boats this summer."

"And make a fortune," Parker finished for his cousin. "I've seen the plans for the Nican Forty. She's going to be comfortable, fast, and beautiful."

"I get it!" Bess exclaimed. "Nican. You took the first three letters of Nick's name and the first two of yours, Andy, right?"

"Not only is she cute, but smart, too!" Parker said, shooting Bess a teasing smile.

Andy chuckled. "This is the Severn River," he announced, steering the Cadillac onto a bridge.

Nancy glanced down at the wide expanse of calm brown water. After crossing the river, Andy turned onto a road that ran near the river. Fifteen minutes later, he was steering down a long drive flanked with azaleas, rhododendrons, and holly trees.

"Aunt Julie and Uncle Robert are happy to have all of us stay at their place," Parker told Ned, Nancy, and Bess. "They get lonely with Andy working all the time."

"They're not going to be lonely today," Andy said. "I forgot to tell you guys—they're throwing a big preregatta party later this afternoon at the house."

"Sounds great!" Nancy said. A moment later, she straightened as the Devereux' house came into view. The stately three-story white brick mansion was set back from the road. A huge expanse of sweeping lawn led up to the house. Andy pulled around the circular drive and stopped in front of marble stairs that led to a pillared porch.

"Wow," Bess gasped. "I feel as if I died and woke up as Scarlett O'Hara in *Gone with the Wind!*"

Laughing, Nancy climbed out after her friend. Ned was already helping Andy and Parker unload the suitcases from the trunk.

"Parker, why don't you take Ned around to the guest house where you'll be staying?" Andy suggested. "Bess, you and Nancy will be in the south wing here at the house. That way you'll be able to look out over the river."

The four teens made plans to meet up in the house before the party. Then Nancy and Bess followed Andy up the porch steps.

When they stepped inside, Nancy stopped short, exchanging an amazed glance with Bess. The marble-tiled foyer was about the size of her entire living room back in River Heights, Nancy thought. A crystal chandelier sparkled over her head, and ornate gilt mirrors surrounded her on two sides. In front of her, a mahogany stairway spiraled to the second floor.

Before the girls could comment, an attractive middle-aged woman with stylish silver-streaked blond hair came walking into the foyer from a hallway beyond the stairs. She was wearing a casual skirt and blouse and deck shoes. "You made it," the woman said, giving the girls a welcoming smile as she approached them. "I'm so pleased you could come."

"Aunt Julie, meet Bess and Nancy, friends of Parker's," Andy introduced the girls.

Nancy shook the older woman's hand. "We're glad to be here, Mrs. Devereux. Your house is beautiful!"

"Thank you." The older woman beamed at the compliment. "Sorry my husband isn't here to greet you, but he's out supervising the caterers. The party starts in an hour, so you might want to settle in before the guests start arriving."

Bess and Nancy thanked her, then Andy led the girls up the curved staircase. An Oriental runner stretched the length of the upstairs hallway. Andy stopped at the second door, opened it, and waved the girls inside.

"Wow! Is this a room or a museum?" Bess exclaimed.

Andy laughed as he set down Bess's suitcase. "Both. My parents collect antiques."

"It's really beautiful," Nancy said, looking around. There was a mahogany bed on each side of the room. In the middle was a sitting area of four wing chairs, all flanking a marble fireplace. Ornate mirrors hung on the walls, and double doors led to a balcony overlooking the back lawn.

"Don't forget, the party starts in an hour," Andy reminded them. "I'll see you then."

After he left, Nancy walked over to the balcony doors. She pushed them open and stepped outside. A large striped tent had been raised on the lawn below, and a band was setting up on a patio by the pool. Several white-coated men and women were running around with chairs, glasses, and trays. A short man with steel gray hair wearing a cardigan and white slacks seemed to be directing the workers. Nancy guessed he must be Parker's uncle Robert.

Beyond the tents, the landscaped yard sloped gently down to the banks of the Severn River. Nancy could see the guesthouse where Ned and Parker were staying. To the left of it was a long dock with two boats moored to it.

"Pinch me, so I'll know if I'm dreaming," Bess said as she came out to stand beside Nancy.

"You're not," Nancy assured her friend.

"Then I'd better find something to wear to the party," Bess said, surveying the activity on the lawn. "From the look of it, this is going to be some blow-out!"

"That afternoon the wind was blowing so hard and the rain was coming down so heavily that I couldn't see or hear a thing! It's a wonder we didn't run aground."

Nancy sat forward in her poolside chair, fascinated by the sailing story that Nick Lazlo was telling her, Bess, Parker, and Ned. Nick was already there when the teens had gone out to the lawn an hour earlier. After Nancy, Bess, and Ned had met Andy's father, they'd been introduced to Nick Lazlo. Since then, they hadn't stopped talking to him.

Nancy thought Nick looked every bit the sailor. Tall, lean, and handsome, he already had a dark tan, and squint lines surrounded his light blue eyes. He was dressed in white denims, a long-sleeved blue denim shirt, and deck shoes.

"So what did you do?" Bess asked breathlessly. She leaned forward, smoothing the skirt of her pink minidress.

Nick shrugged. "We pulled down the spinnaker, reefed the mainsail, and won the race! But only because most of the other boats got lost or quit," he added with a chuckle.

"Uh, are you girls ready for lobster and crab cakes yet?" Parker interrupted. He and Ned were standing behind Nancy and Bess, holding plastic cups of punch.

Nancy jumped up from the lounge chair she'd been sitting on. "Oh, sorry. I'd almost forgotten about food."

"Me, too, if you can believe it." Bess added. "But now that you mention lobster . . ."

"You guys better sample the Devereux' great food, then," Nick suggested. "I'm glad I'll have you along to crew on Sunday," he added. "Hey, maybe we should take the *Skipper's Surprise* out for a trial run tomorrow. We can pack a picnic and make a day of it."

"Sounds like fun," Bess and Nancy chorused.

Nick crossed his arms over his chest and glanced around. "Now I've got to find some rival skippers so I can razz them about how I'm going to win the regatta." He strode off in the direction of the tent.

"He's got some wild stories," Parker said. "It's no wonder, though. Nick and Andy have both been sailing since they were kids."

"Mmm," Ned said distractedly, glancing toward the buffet tables. "Let's get something to eat and then enjoy the band."

"Good idea," Nancy agreed. "How about if I get some drink refills?" She started to gather her friends' empty cups. "I'll meet you at the buffet."

"I'll help," Ned offered.

As they started toward the tent-covered bar area, Ned took two of the cups so he could hold her hand. "Ah, alone at last," he whispered.

Nancy stood on tiptoe to press a quick kiss to his lips. "Sorry if I got preoccupied by all those racing stories. The people here seem really serious about Sunday's race."

"Mm-hmm," Ned agreed. "Maybe we're not expert enough to crew for Andy and Nick. After all, it isn't just the race they want to win, they also want the publicity and recognition for their boat."

"I was thinking the same thing," Nancy said as they approached the bar. When she handed the glasses to the bartender, a loud voice behind the tent caught her attention.

"The *Surprise* is going to be so far ahead, you won't be able to catch her," Nick Lazlo was boasting. Nancy put a hand on Ned's arm. When he turned to look at her, she held a finger to her lips and nodded toward the back of the tent.

"Oh yeah, Lazlo? Just wait," another voice growled. "Your Nican Forty's no big deal."

Nancy's eyes widened at the person's angry tone. "I'm sick of listening to you boast that you're going to beat everyone, Lazlo. In fact, I'll do anything to make sure you don't win. *Anything!*"

Chapter

Two

Nancy stood still, waiting to hear more. What did the angry person mean when he said he'd do *anything* to keep Lazlo from winning? And who was the person?

"What's going on?" Ned whispered.

Nancy gave a bewildered shrug, then picked up two cups of punch. By now the voices had fallen silent. Curious, she walked toward the end of the tent to see if she could catch a glimpse of Lazlo and the person arguing with him.

As she rounded the edge of the bartender's table, Nick Lazlo barreled from the other side of the tent and crashed into Nancy. Punch flew everywhere, splashing on her denim skirt and bare legs. With a terse apology, Nick pushed past her, then disappeared in the crowd.

11

What's going on? Nancy wondered. She stepped over the spilled cups and quickly walked to the back of the tent, followed by Ned. No one was there. Whoever had been arguing with Lazlo had done a disappearing act, too.

"Are you all right?" Ned asked. "Nick almost ran you down."

"I'm fine," Nancy replied. "But I don't think Nick is. Did you hear what that guy said to him? He told Nick he'd do anything to keep him from winning."

"They must have been talking about Sunday's race," Ned said. "Maybe we should mention it to Andy. But right now we'd better get more punch. Parker and Bess are probably wondering what happened to us."

Ten minutes later Nancy and Ned were sitting with Bess and Parker around a poolside table. The band was playing oldies as the setting sun cast golden shadows over the pool.

"Wow. That argument does sound a little more heated than the usual sailing talk," Parker said after Ned and Nancy told him about the exchange they'd overheard. With a shrug, Parker added, "But who knows. Lazlo's always been single-minded about winning."

Nancy picked up a stuffed mushroom from the platter of food on their table. "We noticed. In fact, Ned and I were worried that since this race is so important to Andy and Nick, maybe we shouldn't crew for them. After all, we're not *that* experienced."

Parker waved a toothpick with a meatball on the end of it. "Don't worry about that. Both Andy and Nick are fantastic sailors. They could almost race alone. You guys will mostly be along for encouragement and—"

"Ballast?" Bess joked.

"Exactly."

Bess punched his arm, then dipped a forkful of lobster into butter. "Ah, this is the life."

Ned finished eating a crab cake and scanned the partygoers. "Where's Andy, anyway? I haven't seen him since he dropped us off this afternoon."

"Good question," Parker replied.

"Are you guys talking about me?" a voice asked.

Turning in her seat, Nancy saw Andy standing behind her. Beside him, holding tightly to his arm, was a tall woman wearing a clingy red minidress. She was a thin woman in her midtwenties, with short, spiky streaked brown hair, model-like cheekbones, and eyes that were an unusual gold color. Her lips glistened with bright red lipstick. Despite her flashy appearance, Nancy thought that the woman was strikingly beautiful.

"I'd like you guys to meet Annabel Lazlo,"

13

Andy said as he introduced them one by one. "Annabel is Nick's wife."

Nick's wife? Nancy thought. For a married woman, she seemed awfully interested in Andy Devereux. From the surprised looks on her friends' faces, Nancy guessed that they were thinking the same thing.

"Where is Nick, anyway?" Andy continued. He looked a little embarrassed at the close way Annabel held his arm.

"He got in an argument. We think he left," Parker told his cousin.

Annabel snorted. "That sounds like Nick. He's been itching for an argument all day." Her voice was husky. Squeezing Andy's arm, she nodded toward the bar table. "Andy, why don't you be a dear and get me a club soda?"

"Sure thing. Refills for anyone else?" Andy looked around, but they all shook their heads. When he left, Annabel slipped into an extra chair.

"How have you been, Parker?" Annabel asked.

"Fine," Parker answered.

There was a moment of awkward silence, which Nancy finally broke. "So, Annabel," she said. "What do you think of the *Skipper's Surprise?*"

Slowly Annabel swiveled her head toward Nancy. "I don't *think* about sailboats at all," she replied disdainfully. She looked up as Andy reappeared, holding two plastic cups. "Ah, there you are." She gave him a bright smile as she took one of the cups.

Andy pulled over a chair from another table and sat down. "Nick could've gotten in an argument with half the people at the party," he said. "Sailors are like bulldogs when it comes to their boats."

"Nick did say something earlier about razzing some of the other skippers," Nancy recalled.

"Actually, I wouldn't mind getting a look at this boat Nick's been boasting about," Ned said.

Andy jumped up, a look of excitement lighting his face. "Do you really want to see her?"

"Sure!" Bess pushed away her plate and stood up. Soon only Annabel was still seated.

"I'll wait here," Annabel said, sighing deeply. "Don't be too long, Andrew," she added coyly.

Andy flushed. He definitely seemed uncomfortable with Annabel's behavior. "Maybe Nick will be back by then," he said to her. Then he led the way through the crowd and down to the river.

Nancy reached for Ned's hand as they walked beside Parker and Bess. With a light tug, Ned held her back a little. A smiling sliver of a moon was coming up in the evening sky. As Ned pressed his lips to hers in a lingering kiss, Nancy felt a familiar thrill pass through her.

When they reached the dock, Andy was waiting next to the sailboat, grinning proudly. Nancy had to admit that the *Skipper's Surprise* was a beauty. It was forty feet of gleaming white fiberglass trimmed with polished teak, brass, and chrome. Her two masts stretched upward toward the night sky.

"Wow! I'm going to like crewing for this baby!" Parker said, gazing at the boat. "Andy, I'd say you've got a winner."

"Let's hope," Andy said. "Nick and I have been working on her for a year."

Nancy scanned the exterior of the boat. "I don't mean to sound stupid, but what is it about the Nican Forty that's going to make it faster than other racers?"

"Good question," Andy replied. Squatting down, he pointed to the hull of the boat. "You can't see anything different, but Nick came up with a surface paint that has less resistance. And we designed a new keel that gives the boat more lift." Smiling secretively, he stood up. "But that's all I'm going to say."

"Sounds impressive," Bess said. "Can we have a tour of the cabin? You know, see the important things, like the kitchen—"

"Bess, if you're going to be a sailor, you're going to have to call it the galley," Parker corrected. "And on a sailboat, the bathroom is called the head."

"You'll have to remember there's no right and left either," Andy chimed in. "Only port for left and starboard for right."

Bess clapped her hands to her ears. "Enough! Can we just go down into the *galley*, please?"

"Okay, everyone on board for a tour," Andy said, taking Bess's hand. "Ms. Marvin," he said in a mock formal voice. "To board, step over the lifeline—that's the line of rope in front of you— and grab hold of the shroud." He pointed to two taut wires that angled down from the top of the boat's mast and attached the mast to the deck. "Then jump onto the deck."

Bess nodded. With a boost from Ned, she stepped over the lifeline, which ran around the edge of the deck. Reaching forward, she grasped the shroud and swung her other leg over the lifeline.

Suddenly Nancy heard an ominous groan above her. Stepping back, she looked up into the night sky. With a start, she realized that the main mast was tilting slightly to the left!

Nancy opened her mouth to warn Andy. But before she could, the mast came hurtling through the air—straight at Ned's head!

Chapter
Three

"NED, LOOK OUT!" Nancy screamed. She dove for him, catching hold of his shirt and yanking him backward. The two of them fell flat onto the dock, and Nancy felt her breath knocked out of her.

A split second later, the mast crashed across the deck of the boat and onto the dock with a thunderous whack, narrowly missing the two of them. Wires slapped against Nancy's arms and legs, stinging her. She scrambled sideways and bumped into Ned's shoulder. He pulled her to his chest and hugged her tight.

"Are you okay?" he gasped into her hair.

Numbly, she nodded. "Yes. What about you?"

He caught his breath. "All in one piece, thanks to you."

"Hey!" An anxious cry from the boat made

them both look up. Bess and Andy were waving from the starboard deck. "Everyone all right?"

Nancy nodded as she looked at the boat. The mast had ripped through part of the sailboat's lifeline. The boom had fallen with the mast, hitting with such force that it had dented one section of the metal rail.

"Are you guys okay?" Parker called. He was standing safely on the other side of the fallen mast, but his face was pale.

"Yeah," Ned replied.

As he and Nancy got up, Nancy was relieved to see that the people at the party were too busy laughing and talking to notice the accident. Nodding toward the fallen mast, she asked Andy, "What happened?"

Andy was stooped on the deck of the *Skipper's Surprise,* inspecting the damage. "I'm not sure," he replied. "But whatever it was, it shouldn't have happened. Masts don't just fall by themselves."

"It was all my fault!" Bess exclaimed. Nancy, Ned, Parker, and Andy all swung to look at her. Bess was sitting on the top of the cabin, which was slightly raised from the deck. Her face was pale. "I must have pulled the mast down when I grabbed those shroud things."

"No way, Bess," Andy said. "The wires are held taut by the turnbuckle—that's the fitting you screw the shroud lines into. The lines don't come loose, unless . . ."

19

His voice trailed off. Frowning, Andy climbed over the top of the cabin and bent down on the other side of the boat.

Ned and Nancy glanced at each other. "What's going on?" Nancy wondered out loud. Holding on to Ned's shoulder, she jumped onto the deck to see what Andy was doing. He was fiddling with the U-shaped clamp that attached the turnbuckle to the deck. When he looked up at her, his face was white.

"Somebody deliberately unscrewed the turnbuckle," he said in a low voice. "That means the shroud lines were barely supporting the mast on this side. When Bess pulled on the lines on the opposite side, the mast fell over."

By now Parker, Ned, and Bess were clustered around Nancy and Andy. "See, it *was* my fault," Bess repeated, looking miserable.

Parker put his arm around her shoulder. "Anyone boarding the boat could have grabbed the shroud lines."

"Even Nick Lazlo," Nancy said. "Maybe this is what the person arguing with him meant by saying he'd do anything to win." She hesitated, then added, "Though to be honest, I couldn't tell for certain if the voice was a man's or a woman's."

Andy stood up. "Nick *is* usually the one fooling with the boat. This is the first time I've been on it for a week. But why would someone want to hurt him?"

"I don't know." Nancy took one last look at the turnbuckle, then straightened. "But if you're saying that the turnbuckle was deliberately unscrewed, then it couldn't have been an accident."

"I don't know how else to explain it," Andy said. "Nick would never do anything this sloppy or dangerous."

Ned gave Nancy a probing look. "So you think this was meant for Nick?"

"After hearing that threat, it would make sense. After all, a mast falling on your head would certainly keep you from winning the race."

"I don't know, Nancy," Parker said doubtfully. "I think the argument you and Ned heard at the party was just hot air. The mast falling is serious."

Nancy took a deep breath. "That's what worries me. If this was no accident, then whoever loosened the shroud must have been deadly serious. I think we'd better warn Nick."

The group headed back up to the party. When they didn't see Nick, Parker and Bess volunteered to check the house. Andy, Ned, and Nancy found Annabel stretched out on a cushioned lawn chair by the pool.

"The mast fell?" Annabel asked after Andy explained what had happened. Her eyes brightened with the first glimmer of interest Nancy had seen all night. "Too bad I wasn't there. It would've livened up this dull party."

21

Andy let out an exasperated sigh. "This is serious, Annabel. Someone could've been hurt."

"Like me," Ned added soberly.

Nancy was curious about Annabel's reaction. The mast could have fallen on her husband, yet she didn't seem at all concerned.

"We have to warn, Nick," Andy continued. "Did he come back to the party?"

Annabel shrugged. "Who knows? I haven't heard any loud boasting, though, so I assume he's not here."

Ned and Nancy exchanged glances. It was obvious that Nick and Annabel wouldn't win the Couple-of-the-Year award. Nancy wondered what was going on between them. Did Annabel hate Nick enough to hurt him and his prize sailboat?

"I'm going inside to give him a call," Andy said, abruptly taking off for the house.

After he'd left, Annabel stood up and ran her long fingernails through her short, streaked hair. "Well, it's been fun," she said sarcastically.

"Annabel," Nancy began, not wanting her to leave so fast, "you don't seem to care much about Nick and Andy's boat."

Annabel snorted in amusement. "I find it totally boring the way sailors slobber all over their pieces of fiberglass."

"But you must have known Nick was an avid sailor when you married him," Nancy said.

Stepping closer to Ned and Nancy, Annabel poked a red nail at Nancy's face. "At least Nick is a *real* sailor. But all these other people?" Annabel waved at the crowd. "After twenty years of boating with my father, I can sail rings around them!"

For a second, Annabel's golden eyes narrowed. Then her face fell back into its bored mask. "But who wants to? Nick's the only person I ever met who could sail better than I can. Too bad he's such a . . ." For a second, Annabel seemed at a loss for words. Then, with a shrug, she turned and sauntered away.

"Wow," Ned said. "What was all that about?"

"Beats me," Nancy replied.

Just then Andy came jogging across the pool deck. "There's no answer at Nick's. I hope he's all right." Stopping in his tracks, he looked around. "Where's Annabel?"

"Uh, she left," Ned said, glancing at Nancy.

Andy looked at Nancy and Ned, then nodded his head knowingly. "I get it. Annabel departed with her usual charming grace, right?"

Nancy laughed. "You seem to know her well."

"I should," Andy said quietly. "A few years back we were dating. Then Nick came into the picture, and she dumped me for him. It wasn't long after that that they got married."

"Oh." Nancy didn't know what else to say. It was obvious Andy had been hurt when Annabel left him for Nick. And judging by the attention Annabel gave Andy, it looked as if she might be regretting her decision to marry Nick.

"No big deal," Andy added quickly. "Hey, Annabel's really okay. She's had it rough the past two years. Her dad, whom she idolized, died. And then, well, I guess she started having second thoughts about Nick."

"Why?" Nancy asked.

"Nick will always like boats, sailing, and himself more than any other person," Andy replied. "We've been friends for so long that I'm used to it. And of course his passion for boats has made him a talented and dedicated designer. But marriage?" He shrugged. "Annabel needed emotional support after her dad died, and Nick was never around."

"It can't be *all* Nick's fault," Ned put in. "She seems to have a mean streak herself."

"She can be tough," Andy agreed, but at the same time, a smile tugged at his mouth. Nancy had to wonder if he was still in love with Annabel Lazlo.

"Wasn't it luxurious having a maid serve us tea and croissants in bed?" Bess said the next morning. "It almost made getting up early worth it."

Nancy laughed. "Mmm. I could get used to living like this."

The two girls were walking down the dew-soaked lawn to the dock. They were both wearing jeans and jackets but had packed bathing suits and shorts in their backpacks.

"Hey, it looks as if the guys beat us," Bess said, waving. Parker and Ned were already on the dock, both dressed in shorts and jackets. When Ned saw Nancy, he gave her a welcoming grin.

The mast had been raised, Nancy saw. As she climbed aboard, she checked the damage. The lifeline had been restrung, but the rail and deck were still damaged.

Dropping her knapsack on the deck, Nancy turned to Andy. "Okay, what should we do?"

For the next fifteen minutes, the teens were busy stowing gear and supplies and getting the boat's sails ready to be raised. At last Andy gave a satisfied look around and announced, "We're ready to go. While we wait for Nick, I'm going to make a run to the convenience store down the road and pick up some sodas and chips." He checked his watch. "I wonder what's keeping him?"

"There's no rush," Bess said from the bow. She had taken off her jacket and was stretched out on the deck. The morning sun was starting to warm the air. Nancy thought that later they might be able to put on their suits after all.

"Some R and R sounds great to me, too," Ned said, slipping off his windbreaker and joining Bess.

Andy jumped from the boat onto the dock. "Okay. I should be back in half an hour. Let's hope Nick's here by then."

But when Andy returned, Nick still hadn't shown up. Andy went into the guest house to call. When he returned, he was frowning. "I woke Annabel up. She said he wasn't there."

"Did she get a chance to tell him about the mast?" Nancy asked.

Andy shook his head. "She says she never saw him last night. She vaguely recalls his coming home after she went to bed, but he wasn't there now—I heard her calling him."

Just then, the phone in the guest house rang. Parker bounded up the steps to answer it. "Andy!" he called a minute later from the porch. "It's Annabel. She just checked their dock, and the *Neptune*'s gone. Lazlo's probably on his way here."

"The *Neptune?*" Nancy questioned.

"It's Nick's twenty-four-foot sailboat," Andy replied. "Since their house is on the river, too, Nick often sails over here instead of driving."

"Why don't we motor out in the powerboat and see if we can find him?" Parker suggested, having overheard the conversation as he returned to the dock.

"Good idea." Andy led the foursome down to the end of the dock, where a small powerboat was moored. They all climbed in, and Andy started the engine.

The motor was so noisy that no one spoke, which was fine with Nancy. She wanted a minute to think. Ever since Andy had mentioned that Nick was late, she'd had a knot in her stomach. First the threat, then the falling mast. To her, those two things added up to trouble. She just hoped Nick Lazlo hadn't met more trouble that morning.

Andy headed downriver, picking up speed. "There's his boat!" Andy suddenly shouted from behind the powerboat's steering wheel. Nancy stood up next to him and gazed in the direction he was pointing.

A solitary sailboat bobbed in an isolated curve of the river, about a hundred yards from the shore. Beyond the boat, steep, rocky cliffs soared dramatically upward to dense woods.

"That property belongs to Annabel's mother," Andy explained. "It's one of the few undeveloped tracts of land around."

"It's beautiful," Nancy commented. And deserted, she added silently. No docks or homes were visible. If something had happened, no one would have been around to notice.

"I don't see him," Parker added as the motorboat approached the *Neptune*. "It looks as if the boat's anchored."

Ned stood up next to Nancy and put his arm around her waist. "Try not to look so worried, Nan," he whispered in her ear. "He's probably down in the cabin."

Andy cut the motor, and the boat drifted to the stern of the *Neptune*. Parker reached out and grabbed the nylon ladder that hung over the sailboat's side. "I'm going aboard," he said.

"Me, too." Nancy was right behind him.

"Okay. Ned, Bess, and I will check the water and the coastline," Andy said.

Nancy clambered into the *Neptune*'s small cockpit. While Parker went down the narrow stairs to the cabin, she glanced around. A fishing pole lay askew on the cockpit floor as if it had been hastily dropped. A tackle box was open on the seat.

"He's not down there," Parker said, reappearing from the cabin. His mouth was set in a grim line.

Nancy's heart was beginning to pound. Where *was* Nick?

As she stepped aside to let Parker up, Nancy's gaze caught on something—and she gasped. Several dots of red were splattered in a jagged line from the tackle box to the far edge of the boat.

Hardly daring to breathe, Nancy reached out her finger and touched one of the still wet drops. When she drew her hand back to scrutinize the reddish brown stain, she felt a shiver race through her body.

It was blood.

Chapter

Four

"PARKER! LOOK!" Nancy held out a shaky finger, pointing to the trail of blood.

Parker blanched. "Something *has* happened!"

"No sign of him in the water!" Andy called as he, Bess, and Ned puttered past in the powerboat. "What's going on in there?"

As Nancy turned to tell him what they'd found, her gaze settled on the wooden railing on the starboard side of the cockpit. There was a splintered hole through the railing. When she bent to inspect it, her hands suddenly felt ice cold.

"This looks like a bullet hole, Parker," she said grimly. "Don't touch anything. If someone shot Nick, we have to call the police."

"Come on, Nancy, this is crazy," Parker protested. "I know you look at everything as if it's a

29

mystery, but Nick probably cut his hand on a fishhook. And the hole is, I don't know . . . maybe a woodpecker decided to have lunch," he finally blurted out.

Nancy gazed at him doubtfully. "Let's hope you're right. We'd better get to shore and see if we can find him. That blood's fairly fresh, which means that if he did head home, we should be able to catch up with him."

She and Parker jumped back into the motorboat and told the others about the blood and the hole in the *Neptune*'s railing.

"Oh, no!" Andy said in a tight voice. "Nick's house is just around the bend. Annabel's parents gave them the property when they got married."

Nancy glanced over at her friends. Bess's face had turned white, and Ned was still frowning in disbelief.

"A bullet hole?" Ned repeated, looking at Nancy. "Do you really think someone shot at him from that far away?" He waved toward the deserted cliff. "It's over a hundred yards."

"It's possible. Or the person could have fired from another boat," Nancy said.

Andy pounded his fist against the steering wheel. "That's crazy! People around here don't shoot each other. He'll be at home, you'll see." He gunned the motor, and with a lurch, the powerboat continued down the Severn River.

They reached the Lazlos' small dock ten minutes later. The property was bordered by the same sheer cliffs they'd seen near the *Neptune*. Wooden steps zigzagging up the side appeared to be the only way up. As they neared the dock, Ned grabbed a piling while Parker tossed a rope over it. Then they all stepped out of the boat.

The five climbed the stairs in silence. At the top, they stepped onto a manicured lawn. Daffodils, tulips, and dogwood trees bloomed in a well-tended garden on one side of a brick and stone house.

"Come on." Andy started for the house at a jog, with Nancy and the others right behind him. They leapt up stone steps to a brick terrace.

"Annabel!" Andy shouted, halting at the french doors and pounding on the glass. "It's Andy." When there was no answer, he turned the knob and went in, the others following right behind.

"Annabel!" he called again.

With hurried strides, Andy went into what looked like a family room and disappeared through a doorway. Nancy could hear him calling Annabel's name.

Looking around, Nancy saw that the room was beautifully furnished in soft, white leather easy chairs as well as antiques. Cut flowers, plants, and several wall hangings added color. Still, the room was so perfectly arranged and uncluttered that it looked as if no one lived there.

From another part of the house, the teens could hear Annabel's muffled voice and Andy's urgent one. Then Andy and Annabel came into the living room.

For a second, Nancy almost didn't recognize Annabel. Without makeup, she looked like a fresh-scrubbed eighteen-year-old. Her short hair was soft and shiny instead of spiked, and she was wearing a nightgown and robe. She must have gone back to bed after calling Andy, Nancy thought.

"He's not here," Andy told Nancy, Ned, Bess, and Parker. "I'm calling my house."

"I don't know what all the fuss is about," Annabel said, a note of irritation in her voice. "Nick probably forgot you were sailing this morning."

Andy crossed to an end table, picked up a portable phone, and punched in some numbers. Annabel bit her lip and paced across the rug as she listened to Andy talk to his mother. Nancy couldn't help noticing how nervous Annabel was—and she didn't think it was because she cared that her husband was missing. Was it possible that Annabel knew something about his disappearance that she wasn't telling them?

"All right, Mom, let me know if he does show up," Andy finished. After saying goodbye, he hung up. His eyes darted first to Annabel, then to the others.

"Looks like we call the police," he said tersely. "There's no sign of Nick."

* * *

"That Detective O'Reilly grilled me like a potential murderer," Bess grumbled later that afternoon.

"It wasn't just you," Parker said, squeezing her arm. "That other cop, Detective Wilkes, interrogated me, and he was no charm school graduate, either."

The two were sitting on the cockpit seat of the *Skipper's Surprise,* a plate of sandwiches between them. Andy was at the wheel, Nancy was perched nearby on the deck, and Ned was keeping an eye on the sails. The sailboat was just finishing its practice run. The waters were calm, and the sun was bright and hot, but the normally enthusiastic group was subdued.

Two Annapolis detectives had shown up at the Lazlos' house after Andy called the police that morning. They had questioned everyone in the group separately, and it was early afternoon before they were done. Despite everyone's somber mood, the group had decided to take the *Skipper's Surprise* out for a test run. Still, the conversation kept turning back to Lazlo's disappearance and the police investigation.

"Since the police found that gun hidden in the bushes on top of the cliff where we found Lazlo's boat," Nancy explained, "they're treating it as if it's a homicide, even if they didn't find a body."

"I bet the Coast Guard divers turn up something soon," Ned put in as he stood, ready to man the sails. "Plus all those crime lab guys swarming the *Neptune* after we towed it to the dock must have found some evidence, too."

Nancy took a sip of her cold soda. "Homicide detectives tend to think of everyone as a potential murderer," she added. "It wasn't personal, guys." She cast a worried glance at Andy, who was absently steering the *Skipper's Surprise* through the water. She wondered how he was taking it. He and Nick had known each other a long time.

Andy sighed. "I think I really might be in trouble, though," he said, looking at Nancy. "You know when I left to go to the convenience store?"

Nancy realized what he was getting at. "Oh, no! You don't have an alibi for that period of time."

He nodded grimly.

"But you weren't gone more than half an hour," Parker protested.

Andy shrugged. "That's enough time to kill someone. The worst thing is, the road to the store goes right past that stretch of woods by the river. I know what the police were thinking—that I drove to the deserted woods, sneaked out to the cliff, and shot my partner."

"That's crazy!" Parker and Bess both exclaimed.

"The clerk at the store must have seen you," Nancy said.

"Sure. Some kid who was watching TV while I paid him. Great witness he'll make."

"You don't have any reason to shoot Nick," Nancy said. "The police must realize that."

"That's right!" Parker exclaimed.

"Uh . . ." Andy hesitated. "That's not exactly true. I mean, I *didn't* have a reason, but the police might not see it that way."

"Maybe you'd better explain," Nancy said.

Andy took a deep breath as he steered. "Well, like I said at the party, Annabel and I used to date. And lately, since Annabel and Nick have been having, um, some problems, she's been spending a lot of time with me." Abruptly, he raised one hand as if expecting a reaction. "But we're just friends. And nothing's been behind Nick's back."

"Only the police might not see it that way," Nancy said.

"Right," Andy agreed. "Annabel's going through a tough time, and she needs a friend. Nick's made no secret that he wants a divorce. But she won't divorce him because he'd get half of the property her family gave them and probably some of her money, too."

"I'd say that gives Annabel a good reason to want to get rid of her husband," Bess said.

"She might hate the guy, but she'd never kill him," Andy said defensively.

Nancy wasn't sure she agreed, but she wasn't

going to say that out loud. Not only did Annabel have a motive, but she was also the one most likely to know Nick's movements. Annabel knew enough about sailboats to rig the mast, too. And she knew her husband well enough to guess that he'd show off the *Skipper's Surprise* at the party. No wonder she hadn't wanted to join them for a tour. Then, when the falling mast hadn't done Nick in, she followed him this morning and . . .

"At least if Annabel looks guilty, it might take some of the heat off you," Ned suggested to Andy.

"Except, um, there's one more thing," Andy said.

Parker groaned. "Something else?"

"Recently, when I was checking the account books, I noticed that there were three five-thousand-dollar payments to Steele Lumber in one month," Andy began. "Well, I'd never heard of Steele Lumber, so I asked Nick about it. He flew into a rage, yelling that if I didn't trust him to write checks, then he'd quit. A couple of employees heard us fighting. When the police question them, I'm sure they'll mention it."

Nancy blew out her breath in a slow stream. "Whew. That's not good."

"You're not kidding." Andy's shoulders slumped as he stared out at the river. "The company's small, so everyone knows everyone else's business. Which hasn't been so hot lately. We borrowed a lot of money to design and build the Nican Forty. If the boat doesn't cut it, we'll be in serious trouble. I guess that made Nick and me pretty tense with each other."

"Uh-oh, looks like we have company," Parker said, pointing toward the shore.

Nancy looked past the bow of the boat. In the distance, she could see the Devereux' house. Four figures were standing on the dock.

Ned's and Andy's heads jerked up. "Who?" they both asked.

Nancy stood up, balanced against the cabin, and shaded her eyes so she could see better. She thought she recognized the two uniformed figures from earlier that day. "Looks like Detectives O'Reilly and Wilkes are paying us a visit."

"What could those guys want?" Bess asked. "More interrogating?"

"Probably," Ned replied. He headed to the bow to get ready to dock.

For the next ten minutes, everyone was busy bringing down the sails and cleaning up. From the terse way Andy barked out orders, Nancy could tell how worried he was.

When the sails were down, Andy let the *Skipper's Surprise* drift the last few yards to the dock. Ned was standing in the bow, holding the bowline in his hand. In front of him, the two detectives stood like statues, their faces expressionless. In contrast, Andy's parents looked worried.

"What's going on?" Andy asked when the *Surprise* was secured.

Without a smile or greeting, the tall, lanky officer, Detective Wilkes, flashed his badge. Then he reached out to give Andy a hand off the boat. "We'd like to take you in for questioning."

Andy didn't look surprised. "Okay."

When Nancy finished tying the stern line, she came up beside Andy. "Is there any special reason you need to talk to Mr. Devereux?" she asked.

"I'll say there is," Detective O'Reilly, the more muscular officer, shot back.

Wilkes put up his hand to silence his partner. "The lab made a definite match between the bullets from the gun that was found on the cliff to the bullet hole found in Lazlo's boat."

"So?" Andy muttered. Nancy noticed that he was nervously shifting from foot to foot.

Stepping closer, O'Reilly stuck his finger in Andy's face. "When we traced the ownership of the gun, we discovered it was registered to *you!*"

Chapter

Five

MY GUN?" Andy's mouth fell open. He stared blankly at the detectives. "That can't be. My gun's locked up at the office!"

Nancy snapped her head around to look at Andy. He had a gun? Why hadn't he mentioned it before?

From the boat, Bess was watching the scene, an incredulous expression on her face. Ned stood frozen on the dock, the bowline still in his hand. Parker jumped from the boat, landing beside Nancy.

"You guys don't really believe that Andy shot his partner, do you?" Parker demanded, glaring at the two detectives.

"Parker." Andy's father stepped forward and put a restraining hand on his nephew's shoulder.

"The police are only taking Andy in for questioning."

"That's right," Detective Wilkes said. "As long as you have nothing to hide, you'll be home in an hour," he told Andy.

"We still want a lawyer present," Mrs. Devereux said in a firm voice, coming up next to her husband and Andy.

"That's fine," Wilkes replied. Then he turned toward the house and waited for Andy to follow him.

Andy's face was bright red. "I guess I'll see you guys later," he said to everyone.

Parker tapped his cousin's shoulder. "Hang in there. It'll be all right."

"We'll meet you at the police station," Nancy added.

"Thanks," Andy replied. Then he started up the lawn with his parents and the two officers.

"The police lab identified the blood in the boat as the same type as Nick Lazlo's," Eric Meisner, the Devereux' lawyer, explained. "So they're assuming one of the shots from the gun they found on the cliff hit Nick and he fell overboard."

It was late evening, and Ned, Nancy, Bess, Parker, Andy's parents, and their lawyer were in the dingy waiting area of the Annapolis Police Department. Parker was pacing back and forth in front of a row of chairs while Ned leaned against the wall by a soft drink machine. Bess and Nancy were sitting on a bench opposite Mr. and Mrs. Devereux, who were perched on the edge of two folding chairs. Mrs. Devereux's face was pale with shock, and she was fiercely clutching her husband's hand. In the next room phones rang and police officers buzzed back and forth.

"But Andy never uses his gun!" Parker stopped pacing long enough to look at the lawyer.

Mr. Meisner nodded. "I know. He told the police he hasn't taken it out of his desk drawer since he bought it."

"This is crazy!" Andy's father stood up abruptly. "Andy wouldn't kill Nick. They've been friends since grade school."

"Unfortunately, the police look only at evidence, and the evidence isn't good," Mr. Meisner explained, his jaw tightening. "Andy volunteered to let the police take his fingerprints. His prints matched the only ones found on the gun."

Andy's mother gasped. "Will they let him go?"

Before Mr. Meisner could answer, a shrill voice rang through the police station. A second later, Annabel Lazlo burst into the waiting area. She was wearing a black trench coat. "Where's Andy? Why has he been arrested? I want to see him!"

She strode over to the lawyer. Taking his upper arms in her hands, she began shaking him. Patiently, Mr. Meisner loosened her grip and steered her to a chair next to Nancy and Bess.

"Andy hasn't been arrested," the lawyer explained. "He'll be free to go home any minute."

"Thank goodness!" Annabel slumped back against the chair.

Mr. Meisner walked over to Mr. and Mrs. Devereux. After conferring quietly with them, he led them out the door of the waiting room and he motioned for Parker to follow. Nancy hoped the lawyer wasn't telling them more bad news. The information about the gun and the fingerprints was damaging enough to Andy already.

Glancing over at Annabel, Nancy saw that she was crying softly. It was hard to tell if she was really upset or faking it. Nancy reached into her bag and offered Annabel a tissue. Without a thank-you, Annabel took the tissue and blew her nose. When she looked up, her cheeks were streaked with mascara.

"Why Andy?" she asked. "What did the police find out?"

This might be a good time to find out how much Annabel knew about her husband's disappearance, Nancy reasoned. After telling Annabel about the gun, Nancy asked, "Did you know Andy had a gun?"

"Yeah, but so what?" Annabel retorted. "Why does that make Andy guilty? I mean, they haven't even found Nick's body yet."

Nancy was taken aback by Annabel's callous attitude. She didn't seem to care at all that her husband might be dead. The question was, did Annabel hate him enough to shoot him?

"Doesn't Nick have any family?" Nancy asked.

Annabel nodded. "In California." Tilting her chin, she looked at Nancy. "I know you must think I'm awful, but I'm telling you, Nick was the most handsome, charming *snake* I've ever known."

"You must have trusted him enough to marry him," Nancy pressed.

Annabel started to reply but then looked sharply at Nancy. "I don't feel like answering any more questions," she stated. "Especially from someone who barely knows Andy *or* Nick!"

Standing, she swept her trench coat around her and ran from the waiting area. Tears streamed down her cheeks.

"What a performance," Bess muttered, getting up from the bench and stretching. "Even the black coat was a nice touch."

Nancy shook her head. "It's hard to tell if Annabel's acting or not. If she plotted the shooting and set Andy up, then she should be ecstatic now that he's taking the rap."

Smiling, Ned sat down next to Nancy and took her hand. "Boy, you sure know how to get to Annabel."

"She did make a hasty exit," Nancy said, looking into Ned's brown eyes. "You're awfully happy for someone who's supposed to be on vacation and is now embroiled in a mystery."

Ned laughed, then leaned down to kiss her softly. "That's because I'm used to dating you, Detective Drew," he whispered.

When his lips met hers again, Nancy was able to forget they were in the middle of a mystery.

"What do you think we'll find at Lazlo Designs?" Parker asked Nancy Saturday morning as he, Ned, Nancy, and Bess piled into Andy's white Cadillac. After breakfast, Andy had given them the keys to Lazlo Designs and his office. Then he'd left to meet with his lawyer.

"Anything that'll help Andy," Nancy answered Parker's question. "First, I want to check out where he kept his gun and see how easy it is for someone to have taken it. Andy also mentioned an argument he and Nick had over a certain account, Steele Lumber. I want to look into that, too."

Parker started the car. "Let's just hope whatever we find clears my cousin," he said.

When the foursome arrived at the parking lot in front of Lazlo Designs a half hour later, Nancy got out of the car to look around. The company was located in a building that was part warehouse, part showroom. Parker explained that the boats were built in the huge windowless warehouse in the back of the building. Through the large windows of the showroom in front, Nancy could see several different sailboats.

They approached the front door, and Parker

pulled out the keys. "Usually Nick and Andy open the showroom on Saturdays," he told the others. "The manufacturing end of the business is open only Monday through Friday," he added, waving toward the back of the warehouse.

"Are Nick and Andy the salesmen, too?" Nancy asked as Parker unlocked the door and they walked into the showroom.

Parker nodded. "Yup. Except for a secretary-bookkeeper and the boatbuilders, Nick and Andy do it all. If the Nican Forty boats are a success, they're figuring on expanding the business, though."

When they got inside, Nancy, Ned, and Bess walked around looking at the sailboats in the spacious showroom. Nancy noticed a corridor with several doors along it and a wider door at the end.

"The offices are down there," Parker said, following Nancy's gaze. "The door at the end leads to the warehouse."

"Did Lazlo Designs build this boat?" Ned asked, running his hand down the hull of a small sailboat that had Lazer written on the side.

Parker shook his head. "No, the Lazer is a popular model they sell. Nick and Andy build big custom-made boats. Obviously, it's a slow process, though. That's why they were working on the Nican Forty. They wanted to break into the market with a fast racing boat that would have a wider appeal."

"Pretty impressive goal," Bess commented. "Are these some of the custom-made boats they built?" She was standing in front of several framed photographs. Joining Bess, Nancy saw that the sailboats in the photos were much larger than the *Skipper's Surprise*.

"Yeah," Parker answered from behind them. He pointed to the two photos on the left. "Those two are boats they designed and built for clients in Florida."

Nancy nodded, then started toward the hallway. "Which one is Andy's office?"

"Third door to the left," Parker answered. He twisted a key from the ring Andy had given her and handed it to Nancy.

Nancy took the key and headed back to the office, with Ned right behind her. When she reached the door, she noticed that it was slightly ajar. Puzzled, she looked back at Ned.

"It's open," she mouthed to him.

It was dark inside, but Nancy thought she glimpsed the glimmer of a flashlight. She slowly reached for the doorknob, but Ned put a restraining hand on her arm. "Be careful," he whispered.

Nancy nodded, then cautiously grasped the doorknob. Slowly, she inched the door open. Then, suddenly, she gave the door a shove and jumped into the room.

At the same time, a beam of light flashed in her eyes. Nancy blinked as a dark figure leapt out of the darkness, straight at her!

46

Chapter

Six

BEFORE NANCY could react, the figure crashed into her, knocking her against the office door.

"Ned! Stop him!" Nancy cried, as the person pushed past her and shot into the corridor. All she saw was a glimpse of a tweed jacket.

Ned put up his hands to grab the fleeing person, but the man shot out with a solid punch to Ned's chin, propelling him backward. Ned cracked his head against the wall and slumped to the floor.

In a flash Nancy was beside him. "Are you all right?" she asked, gently touching his cheek.

Nodding, Ned gestured toward the hall. "Go get him!" he gasped.

Nancy didn't have to be told twice. She jumped up and sprinted down the hallway toward the door that led to the warehouse. "Parker, Bess!" she called over her shoulder. "Someone was in Andy's office and hit Ned!"

"What!" she heard Parker exclaim. The sound of his running footsteps echoed behind her.

Nancy raced for the warehouse door, with Parker right behind her. She pulled the door open, then stopped to get her bearings. A huge, windowless room spread out before her. Tiny emergency lights set into the high ceiling provided just enough light to see.

Holding her breath, Nancy listened. It was silent. Unless the man had escaped already, which she doubted, she knew he must be hiding.

Just then Ned and Bess jogged through the doorway. Ned was rubbing his jaw. Bending toward Nancy, Parker whispered, "There's an exit to the right. The only other way out is a big garage door that leads to a loading dock."

"Let's split up," Nancy suggested. "Parker, you and Bess cover the exit. I'll bet that's how our intruder broke in. I'll hunt around and try and scare him out of hiding. Ned, you guard this door. That way we'll have him trapped."

Quickly the group spread out. Nancy made her way silently among piles of lumber, stacks of wooden poles, and boxes of metal fittings. In the middle of the warehouse was the skeleton of a boat hull. Nancy was making her way around it when a shuffling noise to her left made her freeze.

In slow motion she turned in the direction of the sound. Behind some metal shelving, she glimpsed a patch of tweed fabric.

Bingo! she thought. Crouching, Nancy stalked around the shelving. The person was huddled down with his back to her, peering around the end of the shelf in the direction of the exit door.

Spying a coil of nylon rope, Nancy carefully reached for it, curling her fingers around one loop. She was slowly inching it from the shelf, when suddenly the person turned. Brown eyes stared at her from under a black baseball cap. The man appeared to be in his late forties, and he had a mustache and whiskery chin.

"Don't move," Nancy warned in the firmest voice she could muster. "We have you surrounded. Guys, over here!"

Ned dashed to Nancy's side, and the man looked back and forth at them. He let out his breath in a relieved sigh.

"You're just kids!" he scoffed, straightening. He arched his back and stretched. *"Oooh.* I need to get back in shape."

That was for sure, Nancy thought. He was a couple of inches taller than she was, with a beer belly sticking out from under his sport coat.

"Did you get him?" Parker asked as he and Bess came running up. They stopped short when they saw the man.

Raising his brows in confusion, the man stared

at the four teens. "What's going on?" he asked. "Shouldn't you kids be at the mall or something?"

Nancy glared at him. "We're the ones who need answers. Who are you and what are you doing here?"

"I can explain all that," the man said. He started to reach under his sport coat, but Nancy caught his arm.

"Hold it!" she said. "How do we know you don't have a weapon? Parker, see what he's got under his coat."

The man rolled his eyes. "Hey. I'm just reaching for my wallet. Left inside pocket."

Cautiously, Parker stepped forward and felt under the man's coat. A second later, he pulled out a wallet and opened it. "'Stan Yadlowski, Private Detective,'" Parker read aloud, looking surprised.

"What are you doing breaking into Lazlo Designs, Mr. Yadlowski?" Ned repeated Nancy's question.

"That's privileged info," the detective said, frowning. "Besides, how do I know who *you* are? Maybe you're here to rip off the place."

"I'm Parker Wright," Parker explained. "Andy Devereux, one of the owners of Lazlo Designs, is my cousin. We have permission to be here and keys to get in." Waving the keys in the air, Parker leaned closer and fixed his gaze on Yadlowski. "Neither of which *you* have."

Stan Yadlowski scratched his head. "You got me there," he said. "Look, I can't tell you what I'm doing here without getting an okay from my client."

Bess shot Nancy a doubtful look. "Is he just stalling?"

"No, he's right," Nancy said. "He also doesn't *have* to tell us who his client is, but he will, right?" She turned to him. "Unless you prefer we call the police."

"Yeah, yeah. I do a lot of work for Bayside Insurance. Now, if I can get to a phone—"

"Bayside Insurance?" Ned repeated as they escorted Stan back to Andy's office. "Do they insure boats?"

Yadlowski nodded. "Right."

Turning on the office light, Nancy saw that the room contained a desk, two filing cabinets, and some shelves with books and papers on them. Stan went over to the phone on the desk, picked up the receiver, and dialed.

"Mr. Aquino," he spoke into the receiver. "I'm afraid I have some bad news. . . ."

After he'd spoken a minute, Nancy whispered that she wanted to speak to Mr. Aquino. Yadlowski handed her the phone.

"Mr. Aquino?" Nancy said in a sweet voice. "How about a deal? We won't turn in Mr. Yadlowski to the police for unlawful breaking and entering if you tell us what Bayside Insurance is up to."

There was a pause on the other end of the line. Then a smooth voice replied, "All right. Put Stan back on, and I'll give him the okay to answer any questions you may have."

A few minutes later, the detective hung up. "All right, kids. You've got me for an hour. But how about we do this over lunch? I'm starving."

Soon after, the five were seated in a booth at a local diner. After the young waitress brought their drinks and took their orders, Nancy sat back and gave Stan an appraising look. "Now, what's so interesting about Lazlo Designs?"

Stan took a gulp of his coffee, then grinned lazily. "Why are you kids so interested in why I'm interested?" he countered.

"It's like this, Mr. Yadlowski," Parker said, putting his palms down forcefully on the table. "My cousin, Andy Devereux, is a suspect in the possible shooting of his partner, Nick Lazlo. We want to clear his name. We're not fooling around here."

Yadlowski's mouth dropped open, and he abruptly set down his coffee cup. "When did this happen?"

"Yesterday," Bess answered, stirring her malted milk shake with a straw.

Just then, their waitress set several plates on the table. "One medium burger, one still mooing," she said in a flat voice. "Two fried chickens. Club sandwich coming up."

Stan Yadlowski grabbed the rare burger and

took a huge bite. Bess took the other one, and Parker and Ned took their chicken dinners. While Nancy waited for her sandwich, she watched Yadlowski tear into his food.

"I was on a stakeout all night," the private investigator mumbled as he chewed. "That's why I got to Lazlo Designs so late." He snorted. "If I'd been there earlier, you never would've caught me."

"How did you get in?" Ned asked.

Yadlowski shrugged. "Easy. I jimmied the warehouse door, then got into the office with a credit card. Tricks of the trade."

"What were you looking for?" Nancy asked. She looked up as the waitress finally brought her turkey club. As soon as the waitress left, Nancy bit into the sandwich. She hadn't realized how hungry she was.

"I was looking for evidence that Lazlo Designs was defrauding the insurance company," the investigator replied.

Nancy's eyes widened. When she glanced at Parker, she could see he was surprised, too.

"A year ago, we paid out a big sum of money on a sailboat that Lazlo Designs claimed was lost at sea," Yadlowski explained. "It was a boat they built for some bigwig client in Florida. The client had only paid a deposit on it, so when the boat disappeared, *we* ended up paying Lazlo Designs."

"What's so suspicious about that?" Parker

asked, picking up a french fry. "I mean, that's why companies have insurance."

"Yeah, and we paid the claim. Six hundred thousand dollars' worth."

Nancy jerked her head up. Beside her, Ned whistled. "Wow. That's a lot of money!" Bess gasped.

The investigator shrugged. "It was a lot of boat, and Lazlo Designs pays big premiums."

"So what was the problem?" Ned asked, taking a bite of mashed potatoes and gravy.

Stan Yadlowski wiped his mouth on the back of his hand, then set his elbows on the table and leaned forward. "The problem is that a month ago, the same thing happened. Another one of their boats was 'lost at sea.' Seems a little strange, don't you think?"

"And that's when you decided to investigate?" Nancy guessed.

Stan nodded. "At first we did it all above board. But we were getting some really weird answers from the people involved. So we decided to investigate more covertly."

"You mean Nick and Andy were giving you the runaround?" Bess asked.

"No," Stan told her. "Actually, we were mainly interested in the husband and wife Lazlo Designs paid to pilot the two boats to Florida. About two weeks after they left on their second delivery trip, the wife was found off the coast of Florida in a rubber raft."

Nancy stopped eating and stared at Yadlowski, fascinated by the story he was telling.

"She was half-starved and hysterical," Yadlowski continued. "This time she claimed that the sailboat wasn't lost at sea—it had been stolen by pirates!"

Everyone looked at Yadlowski in amazement. "What!" Parker exclaimed.

"That's what she said," the investigator confirmed. "Not only that, but she said that when her husband tried to fight back, the pirates killed him and threw him overboard!"

Chapter

Seven

FOR A LONG MOMENT, all Nancy could do was stare at Stan Yadlowski. "I don't believe this!" she finally whispered.

Stan smiled, as if amused by her reaction. "Yeah, pirates. Seems pretty crazy, huh? But there really *is* such a thing."

Nancy frowned. "Are you telling me modern-day pirates are out there hijacking boats and killing innocent people?"

"Actually, I've read about them," Ned put in. "They're renegades who sail up from South or Central America and wait for unsuspecting boats."

"Right," Stan agreed. "Usually they go for big luxury powerboats, but they've been known to steal anything that's worth a lot of money."

Bess was staring at Ned and Stan as if they were crazy. "So Blackbeard is still around flying the skull and crossbones and attacking boats?"

Everybody laughed, and for a second the tension was broken.

"Not quite. Modern pirates are trickier," Ned explained. "The article I read said that they sometimes raise their distress flag. Then when the unsuspecting boat comes up to offer help, the crew members pull out their guns and force the other people off the boat."

"That's disgusting," Bess said. "I mean, you can't even go out for a pleasure cruise these days."

"They must go only after boats far at sea," Nancy commented, thinking out loud.

"Right. Usually they try to get somebody in international waters." Stan took another bite of his burger and chewed for a minute. "That really confuses the issue. No one's quite sure who to call for help. By the time the victims get back to port or are picked up by someone, the pirates are below the equator."

"So it's impossible to catch them," Parker concluded.

"Pretty much," Stan said, polishing off the last of his fries.

Nancy pushed her plate away. Her head was reeling with so much information that she wasn't hungry anymore. She wondered why Andy hadn't told them about the missing boats. What else was he hiding? And what, if anything, did the missing boats have to do with Nick's disappearance?

"We're also suspicious because we know that Lazlo Designs has had its share of financial problems," Stan added. "The company has borrowed a lot of money, and business has been pretty slow."

"So you think Lazlo Designs had their own boats stolen?" Nancy asked, taking a sip of her soda. "That doesn't make sense. They would have received a good price from the sale to the clients in Florida. Why risk doing something illegal?"

Stan waved at the waitress for some more coffee. "Pretty smart observation, kid. One possibility is that they found other buyers. So, in effect, they got paid twice, once from the buyers and again from the insurance company. As I said, they needed money. Which is why we're still investigating."

"Did you find anything?" Parker asked.

"I wouldn't know. While I was trying to get into the file cabinet, some blond broke into the office and scared me half to death." Stan grinned at Nancy, then looked around at the others. "Now that I've told you everything I know, what's this about Andy shooting his partner?"

As they finished lunch, everyone took turns telling Stan Yadlowski about Nick's disappearance and Andy's arrest. When they were done, Stan leaned back in the booth and frowned.

"Hmm. So how does this all tie in?"

"That's what we'd like to know," Parker said. "Only we're out to *clear* Andy, and you're out to *get* him."

"Bayside Insurance just wants the truth," the private investigator assured him.

Nancy stood up. "Then let's go. We need to check out Lazlo Designs from top to bottom. Maybe we can find something that will help us all."

"Find anything?" Nancy asked a few hours later, rubbing her eyes as she looked up from Andy Devereux's desk. Ned, Bess, Parker, and Stan Yadlowski had all gathered in the doorway to Andy's office.

After returning to Lazlo Designs, the group had gone over the office thoroughly. They had checked the locked desk drawer where Andy claimed he'd kept his gun. There was no sign that it had been broken into. Finally, Nancy had decided to go through the company's accounting book, while the others continued their search of the office. She had spent the last half hour staring intently at the names, dates, and columns of accounts due and accounts receivable.

"We didn't find a thing," Ned replied. He sat on a corner of the desk. "Not that we know what we're looking for."

"Really." Parker leaned against the file cabinet. "I hate poking around Andy's business as if he's some criminal."

"Just remember we're trying to help Andy," Nancy reminded him. At least that's what she hoped they were trying to do. After talking to Stan, she was beginning to wonder if Andy might be more involved in some funny business than he let on.

"We didn't find much, either," Bess said. She and Stan had hunted through all the file cabinets. *"Except—"* Pausing dramatically, she waved a manila folder in the air. "A file on the husband and wife who sailed the two boats that disappeared."

"Too bad it doesn't tell us anything that Bayside Insurance doesn't already know," Stan added in a frustrated tone. "References, addresses, the contract they signed saying they'd deliver the boat. That's about it."

Nancy reached for the file. "May I see it?" Quickly she skimmed through the contents. The couple's names were Leah and Mike O'Halloran. Leah's current address was in Annapolis.

"What about you, Nancy?" Ned asked. "Those account books seemed to be holding your interest."

"Mmm." Nancy closed the file and turned her attention back to the open ledger in front of her. "One thing puzzles me. I can't find any record of the six hundred thousand dollars that Bayside Insurance paid Lazlo Designs for the first boat."

Moving around the desk, Stan looked over Nancy's shoulder. "The company paid it out some time last September."

Nancy ran her finger down the figures for the month of September. "Nothing."

"Maybe they put it in a different account," Parker suggested.

"Could be. We'll have to ask Andy." Nancy frowned. "I checked out that company Andy mentioned, too, Steele Lumber."

"The one Andy and Nick had that fight about?" Bess asked.

Nancy nodded. "I found three payments to Steele Lumber in the last month. They were all for five thousand dollars or more. That doesn't seem too strange. I mean it does take a lot of wood to build boats. But Andy also mentioned that Nick had been the one to write the checks, when Andy's the one who handles the business end of the company—"

"Look," Stan interrupted Nancy, pointing at the account book. "Here are the payments made to the O'Hallorans. They received two thousand dollars for each trip to Florida."

"Even though they never delivered the boats?" Parker asked, looking surprised.

Stan shrugged. "I guess."

"We'd better go meet Andy," Nancy suggested.

"I think we have some things to talk about with him." Standing up, she offered Stan her hand, and they shook. "Thanks for all your help."

"Likewise." After digging around in his wallet, he pulled out a card. "And call me anytime. Maybe we can still help each other out." With a wink, he left.

After he had gone, Ned reached out and squeezed Nancy's hand. "What now, Ms. Drew, P.I.?"

Nancy once again opened up the file on the O'Hallorans.

"Uh-oh," Bess groaned. "I bet I can guess. We're going to go visit Leah O'Halloran."

"Right, but first let's call Andy and find out how he's doing," Nancy said.

A few minutes later, Parker hung up the phone. "Maria, our maid, says he's down at the dock repairing the boat. He's determined to sail in tomorrow's race, no matter what."

"Maybe that'll keep his spirits up," Nancy said, getting up from Andy's desk. She headed back down the corridor and toward the showroom door.

"So why are we visiting Leah O'Halloran?" Ned asked, falling into step beside Nancy.

"I want to hear Leah O'Halloran's story for myself," Nancy explained. "If she's lying, she might let something slip that will help us."

When they got to the Cadillac, Bess slid in the backseat with Nancy. "But, Nancy, she said her husband was killed. Why would she make up some story?"

"That's what she *said,*" Nancy countered. "But Leah's the only person who witnessed what happened, so there's no one to corroborate her story. Maybe the two made up the whole pirate thing, and right now Mike O'Halloran is sunbathing on the stolen sailboat at some foreign port, waiting for his wife to join him."

Ned turned in the front seat, shooting Nancy a dubious look. "Wait a second. Are you saying that the O'Hallorans stole the boat?"

"It makes more sense than Yadlowski's theory that Lazlo Designs stole their own boats. Plus, the O'Hallorans had the perfect opportunity. They knew Lazlo Designs would get the insurance money. And they could resell the boat and keep that money for themselves. Or maybe they just decided to keep the boat."

Parker looked confused as he settled behind the wheel and started the car's engine. "I still don't get what all that has to do with Nick's shooting and Andy's arrest."

"I'm not sure," Nancy admitted. "Maybe Nick found out what the the O'Hallorans had done and threatened to turn them in. If they were at Lazlo Designs before, they could have easily seen where Andy kept his gun. After faking Mike's death, Leah could have stolen Andy's gun and shot Nick, then planted the gun to frame Andy."

That's *if* Andy's innocent, Nancy added to

herself. The missing insurance money and the payments to Steele Lumber still needed explaining.

Bess rubbed her chin. "But why not just steal the boat and run? Why would Leah come back with some crazy story about pirates?"

"Because if the authorities figured that the boat had been taken to South America or somewhere like that, then no one would go looking for it," Nancy guessed.

"Sounds like a good theory to me," Parker said, pulling out of the parking lot. "Now let's find the mysterious Mrs. O'Halloran and see if we can prove any of it."

Twenty minutes later, they pulled up across the street from a charming Cape Cod house on a quiet, dead-end street.

"I'm going to tell Leah I'm a newspaper reporter," Nancy said, opening her bag. She took out the pad and pen she always kept with her.

"Looks like you may not get to talk to her at all," Parker suddenly said. "Look."

Nancy glanced out the window just as a tall, striking woman with long brown hair came out the front door onto the porch of the Cape Cod house. She was dressed in a black miniskirt and tight cotton sweater that accentuated her curvy figure. After shutting the door and going down the steps, she walked briskly down the sidewalk to a small blue sports car parked in the driveway.

Parker whistled. "Wow. If that's Leah O'Halloran, she sure has recovered from her tragedy!"

Bess punched him playfully on the arm. "Quit ogling and get ready to tail her. If I know Nancy, we're going to find out where our grieving widow is headed."

"Duck!" Nancy whispered as the car backed out of the drive and turned in their direction. She was grateful that the convertible top was up.

Everyone crouched down until the coast was clear. Then Parker quickly pulled the Cadillac into the road and made a U-turn. "I've been waiting for this," he said as he gunned the motor. "A high speed chase!"

"Slow down!" Nancy said. "We want to be inconspicuous, so stay several cars behind."

"She's making a right turn," Ned announced.

With a squeal of tires, Parker swung into the right lane and turned. Nancy and Bess both grabbed hold of the doors to keep from falling.

"Sorry, guys," Parker apologized. "I'm not as used to this cloak-and-dagger stuff as you are."

Several turns later, they were driving on a four-lane highway.

"The sports car is slowing," Ned said suddenly.

Nancy craned her neck to look out the front windshield. Leah's car was just turning right into the parking lot of a seedy-looking bar. It was a low building with a flat roof, no windows, and a crooked sign flapping in the wind that read Kelly's.

"Drive past," Nancy directed Parker. "The parking lot's almost empty. If we pull in after her, she'll see us."

Parker steered the car into the left lane. "There's a turnaround. I can swing back."

Twisting in her seat, Nancy looked out the back window in time to see Leah pull into a parking space. Parker made a U-turn, and when they were almost opposite the bar, he pulled onto the right side of the road and stopped on the shoulder.

"Now someone else is turning into the lot," Bess said excitedly. "It's a van."

Quickly Nancy pulled a pair of small binoculars from her shoulder bag. She was glad she had packed them for the sailing trip. Focusing, she trained the binoculars on Leah's car. The brunette was getting out just as the van pulled opposite her.

With a big smile, Leah approached the driver's side of the van. The door opened, and a man stepped out. Long black hair stuck out from the back of the baseball cap he was wearing, and a dark, heavy beard and mustache covered most of his face. He had on a leather motorcycle jacket and jeans.

Nancy could hear Bess gasp as Leah and the man embraced. Arm in arm, the two strolled to the door of the bar and went in.

66

Slowly Nancy lowered the glasses.

"Did you *see* that!" Bess exclaimed. "Her husband's only been dead a month, and she's meeting some other guy!"

"That *is* pretty suspicious," Ned added.

Nancy nodded. "That's for sure. If you ask me, Leah O'Halloran is no grieving widow. She's more like a black widow spider!"

Chapter

Eight

Uh, BLACK WIDOW spiders kill their mates,"
Bess mentioned, shooting Nancy a queasy look.
"Are you suggesting that *Leah* killed her hus-
band?"

"No," Nancy said slowly. "But it sure doesn't
look like she misses him much. Unless—" She
snapped her fingers as an idea struck her. "What
if that man is Mike O'Halloran!"

Ned twisted around and said excitedly,
"Right! I bet he's not on some deserted island.
He's back in Annapolis helping his wife frame
Andy."

"Let's go in and get the jerks!" Parker angrily
threw open his car door, but Nancy grabbed his
sleeve before he could climb out.

"Wait! They'd only make a run for it," Nancy
said. "And then they'll know we're onto them."

"I've got the van's license plate number," Ned said. Reaching into the backseat, he took the pad and pen from Nancy and jotted the number down. "Let's call Yadlowski and give him the number. I bet he can trace it in no time."

"Good idea," Nancy agreed. "Then we'll know who Mr. Mysterious is. If we can prove he's Mike O'Halloran, we may have something to take to the police."

That evening, the Devereux' maid, Maria, prepared a buffet on the terrace. Nancy piled her plate with crab cakes, hot rolls, and several different kinds of salad, then sat down next to Ned at the table. Bess sat down on her other side.

"Look at that view," Bess said dreamily, nodding her head toward the river. The masts of the *Skipper's Surprise* were silhouetted against the setting sun.

"Perfect weather for tomorrow's race," Andy said as he set his plate on the table across from Nancy.

"The race!" Mrs. Devereux exclaimed from the buffet table, where she and Mr. Devereux were serving themselves. "How can you even think about that at a time like this?"

Andy chuckled. "That's *all* I think about, Mom. Being in that grimy police station makes you really appreciate things like the wind blowing through your hair."

Mr. Devereux cleared his throat and looked at

the table of young people. "I hate to put a damper on this festive occasion, but this old worrywart would like to find out what you young folks discovered that might help Andy."

"Okay." Nancy, Ned, Parker, and Bess took turns explaining about Stan Yadlowski, Bayside Insurance, and the missing boats. Then Nancy told Andy and his parents about their theory that Nick Lazlo had discovered that Leah and Mike had stolen the boats. "If that's true, then the O'Hallorans had a motive for killing Nick," Nancy finished.

"Wow," Andy said, running a hand through his hair. "If I'd had any idea that the two incidents were related, I would've told the police and you guys about the missing boats."

"Did you know that Bayside Insurance was investigating?" Nancy asked.

Andy nodded, as he took a bite of a crab cake. "Yes, but I thought they were just investigating the O'Hallorans," he explained.

"One more thing," Nancy said. "When we looked at the account books at your office, we thought it was strange that there wasn't any record of the first insurance claim money that was paid out."

"Oh, that's easy to explain," Andy said. "Nick suggested we put in into a separate account that paid higher interest. We figured we could use it to pay off debts if the Nican Forty didn't pan out."

"So, Nancy, as you can see, Andy knew all

about Bayside Insurance," Mr. Devereux added calmly. He was sitting next to his wife at the end of the table. "We *all* thought that Bayside was suspicious only of the O'Hallorans. Still, I suppose we should have mentioned their investigation to the police and to Andy's lawyer."

Nancy nodded. "I hope you'll do that tomorrow."

"I won't have time," Andy said. "Tomorrow I've got one thing on my mind—the race. The Nican Forty has to prove itself, or I'm afraid Lazlo Designs will go under. Especially since it sounds as if Bayside Insurance might not pay our second claim."

Ned had been silently eating his food while the others discussed the case. Suddenly he put down his fork and asked, "Do you really think we have a chance to win the race without Nick?" He waved a hand toward Nancy, Bess, and himself. "I mean, none of us has any racing experience."

"We *have* to win," Andy said determinedly. "We need that race to help promote the boat. Just because Nick's not here doesn't mean I'm giving up."

Parker smiled, clapping his cousin on the shoulder. "That's the spirit. Only I'm afraid you're going to need more than spirit to win the race. Without Nick as skipper, we may not have a chance."

"Andy!" A shout from inside the house interrupted Parker. A moment later Annabel Lazlo opened the sliding door to the patio and ran across the bricks. After saying a general hello to the group, she turned her attention to Andy. "How did it go this morning? Did your lawyer convince the police that you couldn't hurt a flea, much less kill Nick?"

"The police still haven't found Nick's body," Nancy pointed out, wondering what Annabel was doing there. "They haven't determined for sure that he was murdered, so they couldn't book Andy."

Annabel shot Nancy a knowing look. "Oh, he's dead all right. Otherwise, he'd still be hanging around trying to con me out of my money."

"Annabel!" Mrs. Devereux exclaimed. "You're talking about your husband!"

Annabel snorted. "As if he ever cared."

With an irritated expression, Andy stood up. "Enough about Nick and the shooting. I invited Annabel over because she's going on a practice sail with us tonight."

"We're going to need a *lot* of practice if we're going to win tomorrow," Parker added.

"Of course we'll win!" Annabel set her hands on her hips and glared at the group. "We don't need Nick. I told you before that I can sail rings around all those so-called sailors. Well, it's time I proved it. Tomorrow I'm going to skipper the *Skipper's Surprise,* so get ready for the race of your life!"

* * *

"How steady is the wind?" Andy called from the deck of the *Skipper's Surprise* an hour and a half later. He took another turn on the winch that tightened the mainsail, then looked expectantly at Annabel, who was behind the wheel.

"Holding fine!" Annabel called back. "We should have smooth going right to the City Dock."

While Andy and Annabel handled the sailing, Bess, Parker, Nancy, and Ned were relaxing on the foredeck, enjoying the cool breeze. It was after eight, and the moon had risen, sending shimmering gold highlights across the Severn River.

This was the first chance they'd had to relax since setting sail an hour earlier. Andy and Annabel had worked everyone hard, testing them, and they'd passed. Now it was time to enjoy the night.

"This is the life," Ned said, squeezing Nancy's hand. They were sitting close together, their legs stretched out on the bow. Lights from the shore twinkled in the distance, and all they could hear was the slap of water against the boat's hull.

Nancy leaned back against Ned and shut her eyes. "I can see why someone would sell their house, quit their job, buy a boat, and sail around the world," she murmured.

She looked up to see that Annabel was gesturing toward them. "Get ready to lower the sails!"

"Captain Bligh has spoken," Ned joked in a low voice.

Clapping her hand to her mouth, Nancy suppressed her laughter. Annabel was proving to be a tough skipper, but Nancy could tell she was also a skilled sailor. While they sailed, Nancy had seen a few special looks pass between Annabel and Andy. Nancy wasn't sure what Andy saw in Annabel, but she couldn't help feeling sad that things couldn't work out between the two of them.

When the sails were down, the group motored into the narrow channel of the Annapolis City Dock. Sailboats were moored on both sides of the concrete bulkhead that lined the channel. Annabel steered the *Skipper's Surprise* into an empty slip. After they had secured the boat to a piling, the group got out and started to look for a place where they could get some sodas.

"City Dock was once the colonial port," Andy told them as they walked past a row of quaint shops. "It was surrounded by warehouses and taverns."

Annabel shot him a big smile, then pointed to a long, one-story building. "That's the Market House. It was constructed in 1858," she told the others. "You can get great food there."

As the group started to cross a street, Ned held Nancy back. "Annabel and Andy are in awfully good moods for two people who just lost a friend and a husband," he whispered to Nancy.

"I was thinking the same thing," Nancy whispered back.

Nancy tried to make sense of the situation. If Nick *was* dead, Annabel had gotten rid of a husband she hated without a messy divorce. But what about Andy? There were still a few unanswered questions about Lazlo Designs, Nancy realized. She needed to check out Steele Lumber and the separate account with the insurance money. Leah and Mike O'Halloran were still suspects in Nick's disappearance. But until Nancy could get concrete proof to take to the police, Andy and Annabel were suspects, too.

As Andy directed the group into an Irish tavern, another thought flashed through Nancy's mind. What if Annabel and Andy were working together? After all, Andy had the opportunity and the gun. Annabel knew her husband's habits, and the cove where they'd found his empty sailboat was a short distance from her house. Maybe she'd called Andy early the previous morning to tell him Nick would be at the cove—alone. Andy had said he was going to the convenience store. But maybe he'd already picked up sodas and chips and had them stashed in the car.

A sudden breeze made Nancy shiver. It did make sense, she told herself. If her theory was true and Nick Lazlo *was* dead, then Andy and Annabel were both murderers.

Chapter
Nine

MURDERERS. Nancy shivered as she repeated the word to herself.

"Are you okay?" Ned asked, slipping an arm around her shoulder. "You're trembling."

Nancy nodded. Seeing that the others were waiting for them on the steps of an old brick building, she and Ned hurried to join them. She would have to wait until they were alone to tell him about her suspicions.

"This used to be an inn that offered lodging for seafarers," Andy said as the group stepped inside the building.

Nancy was too preoccupied to pay much attention to the old sailing prints he pointed out on the walls of the tavern. She had to get at the truth about Andy, and that meant calling Stan Yadlowski and asking him to find out more about the separate bank account and Steele Lumber. Also, she was dying to find out if he'd traced the license plate.

"I need to use the powder room," Nancy said as soon as they were all seated at a large round table.

"Me, too," Bess put in.

As the two girls wound their way past tables crowded with diners, Nancy could hear a band tuning up in an adjoining room.

"This place looks like fun," Bess said.

Nancy nodded distractedly. The rest rooms were in an alcove just before the doorway leading to the room where the band was playing. "Great, there's a pay phone," she said, heading for it. "I'm going to call Stan," she told Bess. "You keep watch. I don't want Andy or Annabel finding out." Seeing Bess's perplexed expression, she added, "I'll explain later."

Under the pretense of watching the band warm up, Bess paused at the edge of the alcove. From there, Nancy knew she could see their table.

After pulling out Stan's card, Nancy dialed his number. All she got was the answering machine. She left a message asking him to check out both the account and the lumber company.

When she and Bess joined the others back at the table, a middle-aged waitress with bleached blond hair was standing next to Andy, order pad in hand.

"I sure was sad to hear about Nick," the

waitress was telling Andy and Annabel. Her eyes were misty with sympathy behind her glasses. She patted Annabel's shoulder and gave Andy's a squeeze. "You two must be heartbroken."

As Nancy slipped into the chair beside Ned, her gaze landed on a woman sitting at the bar. Leah O'Halloran! At least she *thought* it was Leah. The woman's back was toward Nancy, and her long brown hair was in a french braid. Still, there was something about the woman's figure . . .

"And to have that tragic thing happen to Mike and Leah O'Halloran," the waitress continued, drawing Nancy's attention back to her own table. "Annapolis has never seen so much excitement."

Nancy spotted the waitress's name tag. "Did you know Mrs. O'Halloran, Sheila?" Nancy asked.

The waitress shook her head. "Not as well as I knew Nick. He was in here all the time. A regular, you know? But sometimes Nick would meet Mrs. O'Halloran and her husband for lunch—business stuff about the O'Hallorans' sailing the boat."

"Oh." Nancy slumped back into her seat. Nothing unusual about that. Her gaze darted back to the bar where the brunette had been sitting, but she was gone.

"Still—" Leaning over the table, Sheila dropped her voice to a dramatic whisper. "It's strange that the police haven't found Nick's body. And you know, it's probably just a coincidence, but Old Bill's been missing, too."

With a conspiratorial expression, Annabel said to Sheila, "That's probably because sharks ate them both."

Nancy glanced sharply at Annabel. How could she be so flip about two people's lives!

"Humph," Sheila snorted, straightening abruptly. "I should have known *you* wouldn't care if Nick was shot," she said to Annabel. Then Sheila flounced off.

"That wasn't too smart, Annabel," Andy told her. "By tomorrow, Sheila will have told the whole town that *you* shot your husband."

Annabel shrugged. "So?"

"Uhhh, I hope someone ordered for Nancy and me," Bess said, obviously trying to defuse the tension.

Parker shot Bess a grateful smile. "How do onion rings and nachos sound?" he suggested.

"Who's Old Bill?" Nancy asked. "The waitress mentioned that he had disappeared, too."

"Old Bill's the town bum," Andy explained. "He's been hanging around the dock for years."

Just then Sheila brought back a round of sodas. "Sheila." Nancy put a hand on the waitress's arm. "You said something about Old Bill disappearing."

"Come on, Nancy," Annabel scoffed. "Don't you ever quit this detective stuff? It gets boring."

Nancy didn't let Annabel's rude comment stop

her. Sheila flashed Annabel an angry look, then turned her back on her. "What did you want to know, honey?" she asked Nancy.

"When did you first notice that Old Bill wasn't around?"

"About four days ago, I guess," the waitress said, putting one hand on a hip. "He used to come around pretty regular for a handout at dinner. Leftovers, you know. Then he just stopped coming."

Andy, Annabel, Bess, and Parker had started talking among themselves about the race, but Ned leaned across Nancy and asked Sheila, "Did anyone report it?"

"No, come to think of it . . ." Sheila's voice trailed off, and she shrugged. "But sometimes he's disappeared for a couple of days. You know —too much to drink."

"Thanks for the information," Nancy said.

"Anytime, honey."

After the waitress had gone, Nancy sat back in her seat and slowly sipped her soda.

"So what's going through that beautiful head of yours?" Ned whispered in her ear.

Nancy frowned. "Things seem to get more and more complicated," she said.

"You don't think this stuff about Old Bill has anything to do with Nick Lazlo, do you?" he asked.

"No," Nancy replied. "As Sheila said, it was

probably a coincidence that the two disappeared within days of each other. Still, I like to look at all the angles."

"Probably Old Bill will show up," Ned guessed, then he lowered his voice. "But somehow I doubt Lazlo will. If his body drifted in the current, the Coast Guard divers may never find it." Abruptly he smiled. "Now, how about forgetting there's a mystery for a while, and enjoying the evening?"

Nancy tilted her head up to kiss him. "It's a deal."

"That tavern was a great place," Bess said an hour later, as she, Parker, Nancy, and Ned strolled in the small waterfront park on the Annapolis City Dock. Andy and Annabel had stopped to talk with friends before leaving the tavern. They were going to meet back at the boat in half an hour.

Some sailboats were moored to the pilings, while others were tied up against the bulkhead. A sidewalk bordered the outside edge of the park. As Nancy strolled hand in hand with Ned, she realized there was no wall or rope to keep someone from falling off the sidewalk into Spa Creek.

"Did anyone notice that woman who looked like Leah O'Halloran sitting at the bar?" Nancy asked when they stopped to admire a sleek sailboat.

Parker shook his head. "I would've noticed someone with a figure like hers," he said teasingly.

With a look of mock anger, Bess jerked her hand from his. "Oh, really?"

Laughing, Parker held his hands up in surrender. "Hey, I was just kidding. My back was to the bar, remember?"

"Mine wasn't," Ned put in, "but I didn't notice her, either."

Nancy shrugged. "Maybe it was my imagination."

"You *are* getting pretty wrapped up in this case, Nancy," Bess pointed out. "What was all that stuff about Old Bill?"

"Hey," Ned cut in. "Here we are in a moonlit park in historic Annapolis. Why don't we do something romantic?"

"Like what?" Nancy asked with a smile, sliding her arm around her boyfriend's waist.

Before Ned could answer, Parker grabbed his arm and started pulling him ahead of the girls. "Wow! Check out that cool sailboat," he said.

"So much for romance." Bess sighed, then glanced behind Nancy. "You'd better move—a late-night jogger's headed this way."

Nancy stepped closer to the edge of the bulkhead. Directly below her, moonlight shimmered on the surface of the water. Several boats bobbed and swayed in the water.

"Let's catch up with the guys," Bess said, starting ahead. "I'd like to see that boat, too."

Nancy started to follow, but suddenly someone shoved her roughly in the back.

"What—?" Nancy felt herself fly forward over the edge of the bulkhead, her arms and legs flailing. She screamed, and then she hit the water. A cold, dark curtain closed around her.

Chapter

Ten

MURKY WATER tugged at Nancy's clothes, pulling her down. Total darkness surrounded her, and she panicked as she realized she couldn't tell which way was up.

Frantically she kicked her feet and stroked with her arms. A searing pain shot through one hand as her knuckles scraped against something rough. Her lungs were about to burst when suddenly a strong arm encircled her chest in a lifesaving hold and began pulling her to the surface. Scissoring her legs, Nancy helped propel herself upward. When she burst above the water, she hungrily gulped air into her lungs.

"Nancy! Are you all right?" Nancy heard Ned's voice behind her. Still gasping for breath, she could only nod. Ned relaxed his hold. With his hands on her shoulders, he turned her around in the water to face him.

Nancy gave him a weak smile. For a second the two held each other as they treaded water. "Thanks!" she finally gasped.

"You guys," Bess called from the walkway above. "There's a ladder on that boat moored next to you." She pointed to the sailboat beside them. A rope ladder hung off the stern.

With a hand on Nancy's shoulder, Ned steered her toward it. After they climbed into the boat, the two of them stood dripping in the cockpit to catch their breath.

"W-what happened?" Nancy finally asked.

"I'm not sure," Ned said. "Bess screamed, and Parker and I turned around in time to see you doing a belly flop into the water."

Nancy shivered. "But who pushed me?"

"Bess yelled something about a jogger, so Parker took off after him the same instant I dove into the water." Ned picked up her hand. "Hey, you're bleeding."

Fanning out her fingers, Nancy stared at them. Her knuckles were scraped raw. "I must have grazed them on the side of the bulkhead," she murmured. A cool breeze hit her wet hair and clothes, and she huddled closer to Ned.

"Nancy, Ned, are you two all right?" Bess called from the dock. She was standing by the bow of the sailboat. Nancy could see Parker behind her, jogging back from the other side of the park.

"We're fine," Nancy called. She and Ned walked to the bow, then jumped onto the dock. Bess slipped off her sweater jacket, and Nancy took it gratefully.

"He got away," Parker said with dismay when he stopped beside them.

Bess put a hand on her hip. "You mean *she* got away," she declared firmly.

"It was a woman?" Nancy asked.

Bess nodded. "Looked that way to me. Her legs were awfully slender and shapely for a man's."

Ned and Nancy looked at each other. "Leah O'Halloran!" they announced in unison.

"Maybe you *did* see her at the bar," Parker added, shaking his head in amazement. "She might have overheard us asking questions."

Bess reached for Nancy's hand. "Do you think that was a warning?"

"Or something even worse," Nancy said. "It's possible that whoever pushed me in was hoping I'd never come up."

An uneasy silence fell over the group. Finally Ned said, "Come on. Let's see if there are any dry clothes and some first-aid stuff on the *Surprise.*"

Half an hour later, Ned and Nancy were dressed in waterproof storm pants and jackets. "Not too stylish," Nancy joked as she sat down on the bench in the *Skipper's Surprise*'s cockpit. "But at least they're dry."

"Tell us again what happened," Andy said, his brow creased with worry lines. He and Annabel had boarded the sailboat about ten minutes after the others arrived.

Annabel rolled her eyes. "I think once was enough, Andrew," she said. "Especially since it was probably an accident. I mean, why would anyone want to push Nancy into the water? Now let's get under way, or we won't be home until midnight."

"Yeah, I guess you're right," Andy reluctantly agreed. "We can talk about this tomorrow, Nancy. I don't like the idea of my friends being in danger because of something I'm involved in."

What exactly *are* you involved in? Nancy wanted to ask, but Andy was already headed to untie the bowline. Her mind was swimming with questions. If Leah O'Halloran was involved with Nick's disappearance, then how did Andy and Annabel fit in? Was it possible that Leah was working with one of them? Annabel or Andy could have tipped Leah off that they were going to the tavern and then to the park.

Nancy shook her head as her thoughts grew darker and darker. Tomorrow they all would be racing together on the *Skipper's Surprise* in the middle of the Chesapeake Bay. She would have to keep really alert—she didn't want to take another dive into the water, that was for sure.

*   *   *

At nine o'clock on Sunday morning, Nancy called Stan Yadlowski before she left for the race. Again she got his answering machine. This time she left the Devereux' number.

"No luck?" Bess asked as Nancy hung up the phone in the Devereux' kitchen.

Nancy shook her head. "I wonder what our friend Stan is up to," she said. "Maybe he's dodging us."

The two girls left by the kitchen door and walked down to the dock. Both were carrying backpacks with changes of clothes, sunblock, and bathing suits.

"Hey! Check out the two gorgeous sailors!" Parker called out cheerfully from the dock. Andy, Annabel, and Ned were already busy on the deck of the *Skipper's Surprise,* unpacking sails and checking the sheets, which were the lines that were used for pulling the sails in and out.

Parker greeted Bess with a big hug, then the three of them stepped over the lifeline onto the boat. From his perch on top of the cabin, Ned gave Nancy a big grin. "Ready for a great race?"

Annabel looked sharply at Nancy and Bess. "There's a stiff wind, so we'll need ballast. That means moving quickly from the port to star-board deck whenever I holler," she added. Turning on her heel, she went to the cockpit and took the wheel. "Okay, let's get under way!"

Ned and Parker reacted immediately by unty-ing the stern lines and bowlines from the dock, while Andy was busy unfurling the different sails. As Annabel started the motor, the two boys leapt back onto the boat. Nancy went to the bow to get the jib ready to hoist.

Half an hour later, the *Skipper's Surprise* was sailing briskly down the Severn River toward the Naval Academy.

"At ten o'clock, all the boats that are racing rendezvous off the channel marker AH-One that leads into the Severn River," Andy explained to Ned, Nancy, Parker, and Bess.

"How do you know what course you're supposed to race?" Ned asked.

"It's pretty complicated," Annabel answered. "The race committee first checks wind direction and velocity."

"Wind direction determines where the weather mark will be placed," Andy added. "Velocity determines how long the course will be."

Bess gave Andy a puzzled look. "Pardon my being so stupid, but what is a weather mark?"

"A big orange buoy. They set the markers in Chesapeake Bay," Andy told her. "The weather mark is the one that's set upwind. Since the wind appears to be northeast, it'll be set by the eastern side of the Bay Bridge. We'll sail to the weather mark first, then head southwest to what's called the leeward mark."

"That should be fun," Nancy said. She was sitting between Ned and Bess on the rail behind the lifeline. Their bare feet dangled over the edge of the boat. Cool water sprayed Nancy's legs, and the wind whipped through her hair. If this was what it was to be ballast, she decided she didn't mind a bit.

Half an hour later, the *Skipper's Surprise* approached a large group of sailboats. Andy pointed out the race committee boat, designated by a blue flag with the gold letters *RC* on it. Spread out in the surrounding area were about a hundred and twenty-five sailboats, their triangular sails white against the blue sky.

"We're racing against all those boats?" Bess asked, her mouth dropping open.

Annabel rolled her eyes. "Don't you know anything?" she scoffed. "There are five classes of boats, separated according to size. We'll be racing against twenty boats or more in our class."

"That's still some pretty stiff competition," Ned said, letting out a low whistle.

Andy patted the boom of the *Skipper's Surprise.* "That's why sailors are always looking for an edge. If our keel shape can pare a few seconds per mile off our racing time, the *Skipper's Surprise* will be a winner."

"And so will Lazlo Designs!" Annabel crowed. "Every sailor in the world will be flooding the company with orders for the Nican Forty."

Suddenly Nancy's eyes widened. The keel shape! Why hadn't she thought of it before?

Holding on to the lifeline, she pulled her legs up and spun around to face the cockpit. "Andy!"

she called out. "Could someone be trying to steal your design for the keel shape?"

"I don't know," Andy said, frowning. "I never even thought about that possibility."

"That's right!" Bess hit her palm against her forehead. "Why didn't we think of that before?"

"Because we were concentrating on why someone would shoot Nick," Nancy explained. "Then Stan Yadlowski complicated things with his story about the pirates."

For a second, the group was silent. Then Parker asked the question that was on Nancy's mind. "Is everyone thinking what I'm thinking?" he asked. "That maybe Stan isn't who he's pretending to be?"

Nancy nodded. "Stan Yadlowski might be a private detective," she said in a gloomy voice, "but maybe he's not working just for Bayside Insurance. Maybe someone else paid him to break into Andy's office to find the keel design for the Nican Forty!"

Chapter
Eleven

SO YOU THINK Stan is pulling a fast one on us?" Annabel asked. It was the first time she had shown interest in the case, Nancy thought.

Andy jumped up from his seat in the cockpit. "Maybe *Stan* shot Nick," he said angrily. "Nick might have found out that he was trying to steal the plans."

"But what about Leah and her pirate story?" Bess asked, confused. "Did Yadlowski just make that up to cast suspicion on someone else?"

Nancy let out a sigh and shrugged. "I wish I had answers for all our questions, but I don't," she said.

Suddenly Parker stood up on top of the cabin and pointed out over the water. "Look, the race committee has posted the course."

Andy gazed at the banner that had been hung

from the race committee's boat. Then he consulted the race circular in his hand. "Just as I thought. We'll have to sail to the Bay Bridge for the first mark of the upwind leg. Then we'll run downwind about five miles to the leeward mark."

"Piece of cake," Annabel said confidently. She steered the *Skipper's Surprise* toward an orange marker bobbing in the water that marked the starting line. "At least it will be if you guys remember all you learned. What's tacking?" She shot the question at Bess.

"Uh," Bess stammered, "that's when the boat changes course, and you have to switch the mainsail to the other side of the boat," she blurted out.

"Right," Parker said.

"The forty-footers go first," Andy said. "That means us. There'll be a warning gun, then a preparatory gun, and then we're off. So let's get ready, crew!"

Half an hour into the race, the *Skipper's Surprise* was nearing the graceful arcs of the Chesapeake Bay Bridge. Nancy had to admit that so far the race had been exhilarating. In front of the bridge, she could see the orange weather mark that signaled the end of the upwind leg. They had to round that mark counterclockwise, then head south to the leeward mark.

Annabel had explained that rounding the mark was the hardest part of the race. All the sailboats were converging on that one point, so the skipper had to avoid accidents yet work for the best position to get ahead.

"Ned, are you and Nancy ready to handle the jib?" Annabel called above the wind.

Ned was braced on the port side of the boat. Nancy was on the starboard side, ready to cast the jib sheet off the winch. The jib was the triangular sail in front of the mainsail. When they tacked to round the mark, the jib would have to change from the right side to the left. Nancy would let out slack in the sheets on her side, while Ned would pull the sheet tight on the port side so the jib would be set for the downwind part of the course.

"Ready!" Ned shouted back.

Positioned at the bow, Parker and Bess were getting the spinnaker ready to fly. The spinnaker was a brightly colored sail that ballooned out in front during the downwind leg for extra speed.

"We're ready to set the spinnaker pole," Parker added.

"Wait for my signal!" Annabel called out. Behind her, Andy was in control of the mainsail, automatically making adjustments as Annabel made slight changes to the course she was steering.

As they approached the orange marker, Nancy's heart began to race. On the right side of the *Skipper's Surprise* three other forty-footers were rushing straight for the marker, too.

Nancy held her breath as she saw what Annabel was trying to do. There was just enough room to squeeze the *Surprise* between the three boats and the marker. Since they would then be on the leeward side of the boats, the *Surprise* would have the right of way and the racer's advantage. They'd be able to round the mark ahead of the three other boats. But if Annabel made the slightest mistake, they could crash right into the marker or one of the boats.

Adrenaline pumped through Nancy as they glided swiftly toward the marker. Off to the right, the three boats angled straight toward the *Skipper's Surprise*. Nancy tensed, waiting for the crash.

"Cast off the jib!" Annabel shouted.

Ned and Nancy jumped to action. At the same time, Andy let out the mainsail, and the *Surprise* shot into the wind and tacked onto the same course as the three boats. At the bow Parker and Bess readied the spinnaker.

"Ease the jib and set the spinnaker pole!" Annabel directed.

As the *Skipper's Surprise* circled the mark and headed south, the spinnaker rose into the air, caught the wind, and billowed out, its neon orange stripes zigzagging across it. Looking quickly over her shoulder, Nancy could see the three other boats rounding the mark about two lengths behind.

"We did it!" Andy cheered. Across the top of

the cabin, Ned gave Nancy the thumbs-up sign. The *Skipper's Surprise* was ahead. If the rest of the race was this successful, they were going to win!

"So what happened?" Bess grumbled three hours later as the tired crew sailed back up to the Devereux' dock. "At first we were winning, and then . . ." Her voice trailed off as she slumped onto the cockpit seat. Next to her, Nancy could see Andy staring glumly out across the Severn River. Ever since they'd lost the race, he'd been silent.

Annabel sighed. "Well, I can't blame it on the crew," she said, giving everyone a reluctant smile.

Thank goodness, Nancy thought. When they'd come in fourth, she'd been braced for Annabel's wrath. Nancy was sitting with Ned on the deck, leaning against the side of the cabin. Ned's arm was draped around her shoulder. The wind, the sun, and the fast pace had drained them both.

"Maybe if Nick had been skipper, we would have won," Annabel said, casting a worried look at Andy.

"No, you did a great job," Andy shot back. "It's the Nican. Something's not right."

"What!" Parker exclaimed, echoing Nancy's surprise. He was standing at the bow, folding up the jib. "What do you mean?"

"There was no way *anyone* should've beaten us," Andy said firmly.

"Do you think someone sabotaged the boat?" Nancy asked.

"I don't know how. I checked her from stem to stern this morning." Andy's angry expression changed to one of bewilderment. "This is all so crazy! And the worst thing is, we may get to shore and I'll find out something else horrible—like that I'm going to jail for the rest of my life."

"No way!" Annabel said, a determined set to her jaw. "There's no way they can prove you shot Nick."

The two of them looked genuinely distressed, and Nancy wished she could believe they *hadn't* been involved in Nick's disappearance. Still, she couldn't be sure. With Stan's possible deceit, Leah O'Halloran's involvement, and perhaps sabotage, Nancy didn't know whom to suspect— or whom to trust.

"Look, someone's coming to meet us," Ned said.

Nancy turned to see two figures moving across the lawn. "Oh, great," Andy groaned. "I bet it's those two homicide detectives."

Nancy stood up and trained her binoculars on the dock. "No, it's your mom and dad, and they have big grins on their faces."

"I hope it's not because they think we won," Annabel spoke up from the wheel. "Bess, you grab the mooring line. Nancy, help Parker in the bow. Andy, drop the mainsail. And, Ned, you get ready to keep the boat from hitting the dock's pilings."

"How'd the race go?" Mr. Devereux asked after the group had docked. "Did the *Skipper's Surprise* leave the rest in her wake?"

"Um, not exactly," Andy replied quietly.

As Nancy jumped to the dock with the bowline, Mrs. Devereux turned to her. "Nancy, a Stan somebody has called twice for you. It sounded important. I left a number by the phone where you can reach him."

Nancy thanked the older woman, but her stomach was churning. That morning she had thought Stan was an ally. Now she had no idea what he was up to. Was he working for someone who wanted to steal the design of the Nican Forty's keel? Or was he helping to sabotage the boat so it wouldn't be a success? It was Sunday, so she couldn't double-check the office of Bayside Insurance. That meant she'd have to be extra careful when she spoke to Stan Yadlowski.

Nancy excused herself and jogged up to the house. She found the number by the phone in the front hall. This time Stan answered on the first ring.

"Hi, Stan." Nancy kept her voice as calm as possible. "What did you find out?"

"Lots," Stan replied in a grim voice. "But I don't think you're going to like it."

Nancy sucked in her breath. "Why not?"

"Because it makes your friend Andy look awfully suspicious. I checked into the account where the insurance money was deposited."

"And?" Nancy prompted, tightening her grip on the phone receiver.

"There *is* no money," Stan replied. "The balance in the account was under a hundred dollars."

"What? What happened to the rest?"

"A friend of mine just happens to work at Annapolis National. She checked the computer for me and said that the money's been slowly paid out to—now, get this—Steele Lumber."

Nancy drew her breath in sharply. "That's the company I noticed in Lazlo Design's account books."

"Right," Stan said. "Lucky for me, one of the checks written to Steele Lumber had just come in the day I visited. My friend pulled it for me." Stan hesitated briefly before adding, "And the check was signed by none other than your friend Andrew Devereux."

Chapter

Twelve

Nancy almost dropped the telephone receiver in her shock. *Andy* had been the one withdrawing the money! But he'd denied even knowing about Steele Lumber.

Just then, a hand closed around her shoulder. With a gasp, Nancy spun around to find Andy behind her, a grim look on his face.

"Nancy! Are you still there?" Stan said over the phone line.

Keeping her eyes on Andy, Nancy slowly spoke into the receiver. "Yes."

Andy's parents strode into the hall behind their son. "What's going on?" Mr. Devereux asked.

"What did Stan say?" Andy asked.

Nancy took a deep breath, willing her heartbeat to slow down. Holding up a finger to Andy and his parents, she spoke to Stan again. "What about the license plate number of the van that met Leah O'Halloran?" she asked.

While waiting for Stan's answer, Nancy tried to reason through what she'd just learned. If Andy was trying to keep the Steele Lumber account a secret, why would he have mentioned it to her in the first place? For all she knew, Stan was feeding her false information. If he *was* working for a rival company or a saboteur, it would be to his advantage to make Andy look as guilty as possible.

Stan's voice came back over the line. "The van's from a local rental company. It'll take a little more time to figure out who rented it. I should have that information and something on Steele Lumber by Monday. My guess is that Steele Lumber is just a dummy account."

Nancy thanked Stan and hung up.

"Well? What did he say?" Andy probed. Mr. and Mrs. Devereux were right behind him.

"From the look on your face, I'd say it wasn't good news," Andy's father guessed.

Taking a deep breath, Nancy told them about the insurance money having been withdrawn from the special account they had set up. Andy's mouth dropped, and his eyes glazed over.

"You don't believe that *I* took it, do you?" Andy exclaimed as his parent's surprised gaze swung to him. His face went from white to bright red. "Someone is setting me up. And when I find out who it is, I'm going to kill them!" Spinning around, he started for the stairs.

Nancy ran after him, catching him on the bottom step. "Andy, wait!" she said. "Stan might be lying. We need to get a look at that account."

"That's right!" Mr. Devereux added determinedly. "The account is at Annapolis National, right? I play golf with the president. He'll help us clear this up, even if it is Sunday."

An hour later Mr. Stewart, president of the Annapolis National Bank, and Mary Masterson, the manager, were standing with Mr. Devereux, Andy, and Nancy behind the counter of the bank. The others had stayed at the house to finish cleaning up the *Skipper's Surprise* and fix dinner.

Andy was staring at a computer printout statement of his account. Nancy was standing next to him, reading down the list of checks drawn against the special account. In the last two months, numerous checks had been written out to Steele Lumber until the balance of the account was only ninety dollars. Photocopies of the checks showed that Andy's signature was on them.

"I did *not* write those checks," Andy declared angrily. "Someone must have forged my signature."

"Uh, the signature would have been compared to your signature card," Mary Masterson spoke up hesitantly.

Andy's eyes narrowed. Nancy had never seen

102

him so angry, not that she blamed him. If someone was setting him up, they were doing a good job.

"Look, why would I drain my own account, then deny it?" he asked. "After all, it *is* my money. Nick or I could move it into another account whenever we wanted."

"So you and Nick were joint account holders?" Nancy asked. A germ of an idea had just come to her.

"What are you getting at?" Andy asked, puzzled.

"You mentioned that Nick had also written out several checks to Steele Lumber from the company's account," she said quickly. "Could he have taken out the insurance money without your knowing about it?"

Mr. Devereux clapped his son excitedly on the shoulder. "Of course he could have."

Andy thought about it for a second. "It's possible. Come to think of it, I don't think I received any statement for this account last month—or the month before. I know this sounds stupid, but I didn't even think about it because we had agreed not to touch it. So someone *could* have withdrawn the money without my knowledge."

"Then that explains everything," Mr. Stewart said. "Nick must have had a reason to take the money out."

Nancy's mind was whirling a mile a minute. If

Nick Lazlo had written the checks, why had he signed *Andy's* name to them? And why was he paying out such large sums of money to Steele Lumber?

Absently, Nancy took the computer statement and folded it. Maybe when they found the answer to those two questions, they would solve the case.

Monday morning Ned, Nancy, Andy, Parker, and Bess were finishing breakfast on the patio. The air smelled sweetly of cut grass and flowers. Still, everyone's mood was gloomy.

"Let's try to look at this rationally," Nancy said. "Maybe if we all put our heads together, we can figure out this case."

"I just know Andy didn't do it," Parker declared. "I mean, if you were going to make off with over half a million dollars, you'd at least do it right—head for some remote tropical island so you could enjoy it."

"And you certainly would wipe your fingerprints off the gun that was used to shoot at Nick Lazlo," Bess chimed in, as she finished eating a muffin. "I think all this account stuff is to confuse us. Leah O'Halloran is our crook. Let's concentrate on her."

Nancy silently agreed. One thing she knew was that Andy Devereux wasn't stupid. All her instincts told her that he wouldn't have left so many obvious clues pointing to himself. That meant that someone else was setting him up.

Someone who knew a lot about sailing and the business—someone like Annabel or the O'Hallorans.

"At least we know Stan Yadlowski was telling the truth about the account with the insurance money," Nancy said. "By the way, he called just before breakfast. He said he wants us to meet him at his office—he has some interesting information to show us. So I'd say he's working with us instead of against us."

"Unless the interesting information he wants to show us is a gun," Andy put in.

Dropping her napkin on the table, Nancy stood up. "That's why we're going to pay a visit to Bayside Insurance first and find out for sure if Mr. Stan Yadlowski is who he says he is."

"Not me," Andy said, getting to his feet as well. "I'm meeting a boatbuilder friend of mine at the office so he can study the design of the Nican. If no one sabotaged the *Surprise*, I want to know why she didn't win yesterday's race. You guys can take my car. I'll take my mom's."

"Why don't Bess and I go with you?" Parker offered. "We can go through Nick's office and look for those missing account statements. If we can find something that proves Nick was the one withdrawing the insurance money, that'll really help your case."

"But *why* would Nick do that?" Ned wondered aloud.

"That's the ten-million-dollar question. Hope-

105

fully we'll learn the answer soon," Nancy said. Turning to Andy, Bess, and Parker, she added, "Ned and I will meet Stan at his office, then call you at Lazlo Designs."

An hour later Ned and Nancy stood in front of the door of a small clapboard house on the outskirts of Annapolis. The paint on the door was chipped, and the bushes flanking the stoop had taken over.

"Are you sure this is Stan's office?" Ned asked dubiously. He was stretching sideways, trying to peer into a window.

Nancy nodded. "This is the address."

"Let me knock. If he shoots us through the door, at least you'll be left to get him," Ned joked.

"Not necessary. You may not trust him, but after talking to Mr. Aquino of Bayside Insurance, I'm convinced that Stan's on the level. Aquino confirmed Stan's story about the pirates and about their investigation."

Just then the door opened, and Stan waved the two teens inside. "Hi. I thought I saw someone spying in my window," he said with a smile.

As Nancy stepped in, she looked around with a practiced eye. Stan's house may have looked ramshackle from the outside, but inside it was cozy and cheery. In the center of his living room, he had a state-of-the-art computer system.

"Nice equipment," Ned commented.

"Only the best," Stan said. He sat down in a swivel chair in front of the computer. "People don't realize that nowadays half the work a P.I. does is at a keyboard."

"So what do you have for us?" Nancy asked.

"Steele Lumber's bank records." Stan pointed to a list of numbers on the left of the screen.

"How did you get access to that?" Ned asked.

Stan chuckled. "Don't ask."

Nancy had kept the computer printout from Annapolis National. Now she took it from her pocket and unfolded it, comparing the figures on the screen with the figures on the paper. "It looks as if the deposits made to Steele Lumber coincide with the withdrawals from Andy and Nick's special account as well as the checks written by Lazlo Designs." She frowned. "There don't seem to be deposits from anyplace else."

"That's what I thought," Stan said. "Which means this is a dummy account set up strictly to hold money being taken from Lazlo Designs. Plus, all my sources say there is no legit business named Steele Lumber."

"I don't get it." Ned shook his head. "Why move the money from one account to another?"

Stan leaned back in his chair. "My guess is, it's the only way Nick Lazlo would've been able to move that amount of money without anyone else knowing. A person can't draw out large sums all at once, because he'd have to come into the bank in person armed with various IDs. Plus, since it's a joint account, the bank might call Andy to verify the withdrawal."

"So Nick does it a little at a time," Nancy said. "And if he does it by writing checks to another company—"

"A fake company set up by him," Stan put in.

Nancy nodded before continuing her thought. "Then the bank sees only the check. He probably could have forged Andy's name. And he must also have been siphoning money from Lazlo Designs' regular account, which is why we saw five-thousand-dollar checks to Steele Lumber."

Stan pressed his fingertips together, making a small steeple with his hands. "Right. Now we have to find out *why* Mr. Lazlo needed all this money," he said. "And why he didn't want Andy to know about it." Frowning, he stared intently at the screen. "The only other information this gives us is the name of the person who has access to Steele Lumber."

"It's not Nick Lazlo?" Nancy asked in surprise. "I just assumed it was."

"Nope. I wish it was that easy. The name on the account is Bill Jobeson."

"Bill, Bill . . ." Nancy said. Why did that sound familiar?

"Maybe Lazlo was paying the money out to a blackmailer?" Ned suggested.

Stan shrugged. "Could be. Hopefully, I'll find

out that answer when I learn who Bill Jobeson is."

He spun his chair around to face Nancy and Ned. "I've got some more interesting news, too," he told them, a gleam in his eye. "My sources on the police force say that the placement of Andy's fingerprints on the gun look very strange."

"Why?" Nancy asked.

"Because his fingerprints were found only on the barrel of the gun, not on the grip. The grip had been wiped clean."

Nancy squeezed Ned's hand excitedly. "So somebody else could have shot the gun, wiped his or her prints off, then planted it in the bushes!"

"Right," Stan said. "And since it's Andy's gun, the real shooter would have assumed that at least one of Andy's prints would be on it somewhere."

Nancy breathed a sigh of relief. She was glad all this information pointed to Andy's innocence. "Now I know what our next job is. I want to head back to the scene of the crime. The police zeroed in on Andy so quickly that they might have overlooked evidence to the identity of the person who really did shoot at Nick Lazlo."

"Now, what's the plan again?" Annabel Lazlo asked Ned and Nancy an hour later. "Andy's going to sail the boat to the cove?"

Nancy and Ned were following her along a narrow path that wound through the woods owned by Annabel's mother. Andy had called Annabel for permission to explore the property, and Annabel had insisted on being their tour guide.

"Yes," Nancy answered Annabel's question. "He should be there at about the same time we get to the top of the cliff." Andy, Parker, and Bess were going to moor the *Skipper's Surprise* at the same spot where they'd found Nick Lazlo's deserted boat a few days earlier. That would help Nancy to "re-create" the shooting.

Nancy was glad that Annabel had come. She wanted to see her reaction at the scene of the crime. If anyone had had the opportunity to set up Andy, it was Annabel. Annabel knew Nick would be at the cove, she knew how to get to the cliff, and she knew Andy had a gun. Annabel seemed to genuinely care for Andy, but Nancy knew that criminals could be convincing actors.

Had she been working with Leah O'Halloran? Even though no new evidence had come to light implicating Leah, Nancy didn't want to lose sight of her as a prime suspect.

Nancy was behind Annabel as the three pushed through ivy and brambles. Nancy could hear Ned behind her, grumbling about the brambles snagging his jeans. Ahead of her, Annabel moved with long, graceful strides. With her streaked hair and golden eyes, she reminded Nancy of a tiger on the prowl.

"So what is it you're trying to prove with this little hike?" Annabel asked as they walked along.

"I'm still trying to clear Andy," Nancy replied. "Wouldn't you like that?"

Turning her head, Annabel shot her an annoyed look. "Andy's lawyer will get him off. But if you want to stomp around in the woods, be my guest."

As Nancy followed Annabel out of the dark woods to the edge of the cliff, the sudden change to bright light made her squint. The Severn River stretched out below her. Nancy saw the *Skipper's Surprise* sailing into the cove.

Stepping closer to the edge of the cliff, Nancy looked down. The steep, rocky sides plunged to the shore about forty feet below.

"That would be a tough way to go, huh?" Annabel said, coming up beside Nancy. She had put on her sunglasses, so Nancy couldn't read her expression, but there was a dark tone in Annabel's voice that Nancy didn't like.

Annabel stepped closer to Nancy, so close that Nancy could feel her shirt sleeve brush her arm. Quickly Nancy looked behind her. Ned wasn't there!

For a second, panic seized her. Nancy spun in her tracks, trying to get away from the cliff's edge. At the same time, she could feel the stones give way beneath her feet.

Nancy screamed as she started to slide. Out of the corner of her eye, she saw Annabel shoot out her arms toward her. In that instant, Nancy knew she was doomed. Annabel was going to push her over the edge!

Chapter

Thirteen

No!" Nancy yelled. "Ned, help!"

Annabel quickly grabbed Nancy's arms and pulled her away from the edge of the cliff. At the same instant, Ned rushed out of the woods and hurried over.

"What's going on?" he asked in an accusing tone. Reaching Nancy, he steadied her with an arm around her shoulders.

Annabel lowered her glasses and looked at the two of them in shocked surprise. "You don't think *I* was going to push her off the cliff?" she asked. Then she threw back her head and laughed. "Oh, how funny! Annabel the murderer. I've been called a lot of things, but that would be a new one."

"It's not funny, Annabel," Ned said.

With a shrug, Annabel put her sunglasses back

in place. For a second Nancy could only stare at her. Had the woman been about to push her off the cliff, then changed her mind when Ned came into view? Or had Nancy only stumbled in her panic?

Pulling away from Ned, Nancy looked up at him. "Thanks," she whispered. Stepping toward the edge of the cliff again, she peered down to the cove. Below, Andy, Bess, and Parker were slowly maneuvering the *Skipper's Surprise* into the spot where they'd discovered Nick Lazlo's boat, the *Neptune.* Shielding her eyes from the sun, Nancy gazed out at them.

"Not such an easy shot from up here," Ned said. "The person would have to be quite a marksman."

"Is there a way to get to the bottom of the cliff?" Nancy asked Annabel. In her mind, she tried to imagine the crime. Andy wouldn't have had enough time to go down to the shore, hide and shoot Nick, and then climb back up again. But someone *else* might have shot Nick from below, then climbed up the cliff and planted the gun.

Annabel nodded. "There's sort of a path about a hundred yards to the right. Before we were married, Nick and I used to climb down to the cove to have private picnics." Then she sighed. "That was before I realized he was a shark in disguise."

"Can you show us?" Nancy asked, growing

excited. When she'd watched the police and crime team investigate, they had concentrated only on the area around the cliff where the gun had been found. By expanding the search, there was a good chance she might find some clue they'd missed.

"I guess," Annabel replied with a shrug. "But I'm supposed to play tennis, so after this you're on your own."

Nancy and Ned followed Annabel down an overgrown path. It was no wonder that nobody had noticed the trail, Nancy thought. It looked as if it hadn't been used in years.

"There." Annabel halted, pointing to a wild azalea bush growing from an outcrop of rock. "The path's on the other side of that bush."

"Thanks," Nancy said as she and Ned walked past Annabel.

"Don't fall!" Annabel called in an overly sweet voice. Then she turned and headed back the way they'd come.

"Annabel is one strange lady," Ned whispered. "I wonder what Andy sees in her?"

"It could be that he likes challenges," Nancy replied. "Though I agree with you that she's strange. I mean, here we're trying to find clues that will help Andy, and she's off to play tennis."

Nancy stopped on the right side of the azalea bush. Sure enough, a steep, rocky path angled down to the cove. Nancy bent down to study the area.

"Look at this!" she exclaimed, pointing out an imprint of a shoe toe embedded in a patch of clay. "Annabel said she and Nick came down here before they were married," Nancy said in a low voice. "That was a long time ago. I bet that footprint was made last Friday."

"Didn't the police climb down here?" Ned asked.

Nancy shook her head. "They climbed down at Annabel's property and walked along the shore from there."

"That's right. So then, who left *this* footprint?" Ned wondered aloud.

"Let's see if we can find out," Nancy said with a determined set to her jaw.

The two started slowly down the steep incline, pausing to search for signs that someone had recently been there. About halfway down, Ned pointed out a broken twig. Then Nancy found a scuff mark on a rock. When they reached the bottom, she jumped to the rocky shore.

"The tide would've washed away any signs down here," Nancy said. Turning, she tilted her head back to study the cliff. "Only someone who knew about that path would have even attempted to climb to the top."

"Annabel?" Ned guessed. "She could have climbed down at her property as the police did, and then walked over here. After she shot Nick, she could have climbed up the cliff, figuring no one would ever spot the prints."

Nancy frowned. "But then why show it to us? Unless she thought there was no way she'd left tracks. Except she was wrong. The police can use that toe imprint to get an idea of the make of the shoe as well as what size foot the person had."

As she scanned the cliff, Nancy spotted something odd at the base. When she stepped closer, she could see little dots in a patch of dirt that had collected between two rocks. "I wonder what this is?" she asked, leaning down to study the dirt more closely. The dots looked like little craters randomly sprinkled in the dry earth.

"Who knows," Ned replied, coming over to join her. Turning, he waved to Andy, Bess, and Parker, who had anchored the *Skipper's Surprise* about a hundred feet from shore. "All I know is, I'm getting hot and hungry. Those guys look like they're having fun."

Nancy twisted around. Andy raised his soda can in the air in a silent toast. Parker and Bess were relaxing on the top of the boat's cabin.

"That does look pretty inviting," Nancy agreed. "Maybe we could dive in and swim out to the boat—"

She broke off abruptly. "Dive in!" she repeated. "Ned, now I know what these dots are! They're drips of water that splashed into the dirt. When the dirt dried, it made these little craters."

"You mean raindrops?" Ned asked. "But it hasn't rained since we've been here."

Nancy shook her head. "No. Besides, if it had

rained, then we'd see those marks in lots of places. These drips are just in one area—they came from the person who climbed this cliff." Her heart was pounding in her chest as she grabbed Ned's hand. "Don't you see? The person who climbed up the cliff was wet! He or she had been swimming in the river!

"I bet someone was in the boat with Nick," Nancy continued. "Whoever it was shot him, then motored the boat somewhere else to dump the body. That's why the divers haven't found it."

Ned let out his breath. "Then the killer anchored the boat in the cove, swam to shore, climbed the cliff, and planted Andy's gun there," he said, finishing Nancy's thought.

Nancy pulled Ned toward the cliff. "Come on. We've got to find Stan. With all the information he's gathered, this might sound logical enough to convince the police that Andy's been set up."

Half an hour later, Nancy burst from the woods into the sunlight. Ned was right behind her. Earlier they had parked Andy's car along the side of the road of Annabel's mother's property. As the two jogged toward it, Nancy spotted a beat-up sedan parked in front of the Cadillac. Stan Yadlowski opened the sedan's door and got out.

"How did you know where to find us?" Nancy

asked, puffing for air as she and Ned stopped in front of him.

Stan grinned. "Hey, that's my job." He held out a rolled-up sheet of paper. "Wait till you see what I discovered."

Unrolling the paper, he showed it to Nancy and Ned. It was a computer printout. "This is Bill Jobeson's credit report. It's public record. Any time you apply for a loan or make a credit card purchase, anyone can check this."

Nancy studied the report. There were three columns. The first had the name of the bank or credit account and the date it was opened.

"Notice anything strange about Bill Jobeson?" Stan asked.

"I do," Ned put in quickly. "The guy didn't spend anything for almost two years. Look." He pointed to the date column. "He has a long history of credit—charge cards, a car payment, mortgage. Then three years ago—nothing."

"Right," Stan said. "Until last year. Then all of a sudden, our mysterious Mr. Jobeson starts spending again. And look here—" Stan unrolled another sheet of paper. "This is a list of purchases Mr. Jobeson made in the last year with his credit card."

Nancy looked sideways at Stan. "How did you get that? Or is that another trade secret."

Stan laughed. "Let's just say I have my ways."

Pointing to the last item on the list, Nancy

said, "Look at this. A charge to a rental car company—and it's dated Thursday. Do you think Bill Jobeson was the person in the van who met Leah O'Halloran?"

Before Stan could reply, Ned snapped his fingers and said, "Maybe Mike O'Halloran, Leah's husband, is pretending to be this Bill Jobeson person. We thought Leah might have lied about her husband being dead."

"Maybe the two were blackmailing Nick for something," Nancy added excitedly. "That's why Jobeson is suddenly spending money again— Nick transferred the money into a dummy account under the false name of Bill Jobeson. Of course Mike O'Halloran really set up the account, using a fake identity."

Stan cleared his throat. "Uh, I hate to burst your bubble, kids, but the other news I've got is from police headquarters. This morning the Miami Police Department called Annapolis. Mike O'Halloran's body washed up on shore. It took them some time to identify it, but it was him, all right. And just as Leah O'Halloran said, he'd been shot."

Nancy's mind was reeling. "So if Mike O'Halloran isn't Bill Jobeson, who is?"

Stan shrugged. "My first hunch was Mike, too. Now I don't know."

"Well, we've just discovered something else," Nancy told him. She and Ned told the private investigator about what they'd seen on the cliff and her theory that the shooter had actually been on the boat with Nick Lazlo. When she was finished, Stan frowned.

"It could be that this mysterious Bill Jobeson knew Nick well enough to go sailing with him that morning. But that still doesn't tell us who he or she is and why the person shot Nick," Stan said.

Nancy cocked her head to one side, thinking over the case. "There seem to be several suspects. Let's take another look at your printouts and see if they give us any more leads."

"Good idea," Stan agreed.

Holding up the credit report, Stan pointed to the two-year time gap in the dates. "Sometimes when we see this pattern—where there's a big gap between the times a person spends money—it suggests someone who's established a new identity."

"A new identity?" Nancy repeated.

"Yeah. Some missing persons don't want to be found. Maybe they owe their ex-wives a ton of alimony, or maybe the creditors are hot on their heels. So they disappear. The stupid ones get caught, of course. Because eventually they run out of money and have to reestablish credit or get a job. If they use their own name, bingo, we've got them."

"But the smart ones come back as a whole new

person," Nancy added. "I've read about that. A year or so before the person plans on disappearing, he or she begins to establish a new identity."

Ned put his hands on his hips. "Wait a minute. A person can't just pick a new name out of the air. He needs a birth certificate, social security number—"

"Correct," Stan cut in. "So someone establishing a new identity has to take someone else's identity. Usually they find a dead John Doe— some bum who's in a pauper's grave with no family to claim him. Or maybe they . . ."

Bum. The word leapt out at Nancy. *That* was why the name Bill had sounded so familiar, she realized. Sheila the waitress had told her about the homeless man, Old Bill, disappearing at the same time Nick Lazlo had gone overboard.

"That's it! That's the missing piece of the puzzle!" Nancy exclaimed. She suddenly grabbed Stan and gave him a big hug. "Now I know who Bill Jobeson is. He's the bum who hung around City Dock!"

When she and Ned told Stan about their conversation with the waitress, the private detective's mouth dropped open.

"My guess is someone's out there pretending to be Bill Jobeson," Nancy finished excitedly. "The way Sheila talked, Old Bill was pretty crazy and had no family. Someone could have been using his name all this time. Someone who knew the *real* Bill Jobeson well enough to know he no longer had family, friends, a car, a job. Someone who hung around City Dock and the Irish tavern. Someone like *Nick Lazlo.*"

Ned snapped his head up. "Nick Lazlo! Are you saying he took on Bill Jobeson's identity?"

"Yes!" Nancy exclaimed. "That's why the police never found Nick's body and why we found drips on the path, as if someone had swum from the boat."

"But what about the blood?" Stan asked.

Nancy spread her hands wide. "Easy! Just like Parker said, I bet Nick really did cut himself— except that it wasn't an accident, it was on purpose. After leaving the trail of blood, he swam from his sailboat to shore, climbed up to the cliff, shot a hole in the boat, planted the gun, and then disappeared."

Nancy looked from Stan to Ned, then back again. "Nobody shot Nick Lazlo. He arranged the whole thing himself because he wanted everyone to think he was dead!"

Chapter

Fourteen

THE IDEA had come to Nancy so suddenly that she was still reeling from the shock of it.

"That's why the crime was set up so perfectly!" she continued, waving her hands in the air. "I kept suspecting Annabel because I thought she was the only person who knew Nick and Andy well enough to plan the shooting. But who would know Nick better than Nick himself!"

Glancing at Ned, Nancy saw that he was staring at her as if she'd gone crazy. But Stan was rubbing his chin thoughtfully.

"I think you've got something there, Ms. Drew."

"Still, there's no proof that Nick Lazlo is alive," Ned said doubtfully.

"That's only because no one's looked for it," Nancy replied. The more she thought about it, the more certain she was that her theory was right. "If we go on the hunch that he's alive, the evidence may make more sense."

Ned still looked unconvinced. "But why would Nick fake his own death? He and Andy just designed their new boat. If it was a success, their business would explode."

"*If* it was a success," Nancy said. "You heard Andy after the race. The *Skipper's Surprise* didn't perform nearly as well as he thought she should, and yet the boat seemed to be shipshape. What if Nick discovered that his dream boat wasn't a dream boat after all and that they'd sunk hundreds of thousands of dollars into it for nothing?"

For a second Stan silently stroked his mustache. "But how does Nick figure in with the stolen boats?" he asked. "And what is he planning to do next?"

"Probably only Nick Lazlo knows the answers to those questions," Nancy said grimly.

Swinging around, Stan opened the driver's door to his sedan. "Come on, we'll drop Andy's car at his house. Then we have some things to check out. If we're going to convince the police that Nick Lazlo's alive, we'd better be armed with a lot of proof!"

"Uh, are we all going in there?" Ned asked in a nervous voice an hour later. Stan had parked his sedan in front of a tin shed at the end of an abandoned pier west of the City Dock. The shed's roof was partially caved in, and the siding was rusted from the salty water.

When they had questioned Sheila at the tavern, she had directed them to the shack, saying it was the only home Old Bill had ever mentioned. No one wanted to say out loud what they were all thinking—that Bill Jobeson might be in there, dead.

Before Stan could answer, Nancy opened the car door. "I'm going in, that's for sure. If there's any proof in that shack that Old Bill is Bill Jobeson, it might take some careful searching to find it."

Clutching her shoulder bag to her side, Nancy climbed out and started toward the shed, hoping she would not find a dead body inside. Behind her, two car doors slammed shut as Stan and Ned both jumped from the car and jogged after her. She breathed a sigh of relief that they were with her.

As she slowly opened the shed door, a shaft of light cut into the pitch black of the interior, illuminating a cot piled with dirty blankets. An overturned crate stood next to the cot. Flies buzzed around a half-empty can of tuna. There was no sign of anyone.

Nancy let out her breath.

"Whew." Stan waved the air as he stepped into the shack. "Old Bill wasn't much of a house-keeper."

"Let's do this quickly," Nancy said. She gingerly lifted the blankets and musty pillow on the cot. Behind her, she could hear Stan checking out a pile of junk thrown in a corner. Ned was grumbling about the smell as he hunted around the crate.

Stooping, Nancy felt underneath the cot with her hand. "What's this?" she asked as her fingers touched metal. "Hey, I think I've got something."

She pulled out the object and saw that it was a dog tag on a chain. Taking it into the sunlight, Nancy read the tag out loud. "Bill Jobeson," she said, looking up at Ned and Stan.

"Wow. Now we have positive proof that the real Bill Jobeson is the bum Sheila was talking about," Stan stated. "Or at least he was."

"Do you think he's dead?" Ned asked. He seemed relieved to step back out of the shed behind Nancy.

Stan shut the shed door behind them. As they started for his car, he said, "Could be. I'll call my buddy at the morgue. Maybe he can clear this up for us."

Fifteen minutes later Nancy, Ned, and Stan were on their way to their next stop. Already they'd discovered another piece to the puzzle. The previous Thursday a couple of fishermen had come across the shack and found Bill Jobeson's body in his bed. He had died of natural causes. Since there was no ID on him, Stan's friend had said, he'd been kept in the morgue as a John Doe.

"At least now they can put a name on his cemetery marker," Nancy said quietly.

As they drove, Nancy stared intently at the notes Stan had made of Bill Jobeson's credit card purchases.

"Our bogus Bill Jobeson has made several purchases at the Chessie Marina. That suggests that he's a sailor," she said. "Like Nick Lazlo."

Stan abruptly steered his car onto the side of the road. "Hand me the receiver of my car phone. I'm going to call the Chessie Marina and pretend I'm Bill Jobeson. They might just unknowingly tell us something."

While he dialed, Nancy turned in the car seat. "Maybe by this evening we'll have enough evidence to clear Andy. Then we'll be able to enjoy that moonlight sail Andy suggested." She checked her watch. "We're supposed to meet everyone at the City Dock in two hours."

Ned peered out the car window. "If the weather stays like this, I think it'll be more like a picnic under the clouds." Over the course of the day, gray clouds had begun to cover the sky. Now it was beginning to look as if it might rain.

"Hello, this is Bill Jobeson," Stan spoke into his car phone, bringing Nancy's attention back to his call. "I'm calling about the purchases I made last Friday."

There was a long pause. Nancy watched as Stan's eyes widened. "Thanks," the private investigator said in a level voice. But when he hung up and turned toward Nancy and Ned, he could barely contain his excitement.

"Chessie Marina just gave us the lead we need!" he said. "When I told them I was Bill Jobeson calling about the purchases I'd made last week, they said that the new Sabre Forty sailboat that *Ms. O'Halloran* and I bought would be ready by tonight!"

For a second, Ned and Nancy were too stunned to speak. "Nick and Leah are in this together?" Nancy finally gasped.

"So that must have been *Nick* we saw in the parking lot with Leah!" Ned exclaimed. "I never would have recognized him in that disguise."

"We'll soon find out if it was Nick," Stan declared, pulling back onto the road again. "Our next stop is to see Ms. Leah O'Halloran. I think our 'grieving' widow has some explaining to do."

"No one's home," Stan announced a short time later, joining Ned and Nancy on the front porch of Leah O'Halloran's house.

After parking the car across the street from the house, Stan had knocked on the front door. When there was no answer, he'd walked around back while Nancy and Ned waited on the porch.

"The guy at Chessie Marina said the boat

wouldn't be ready until tonight," Ned said. "Let's hope that means she's still around."

Standing on tiptoe, Nancy looked into the small square window in the door. "This would be a good time to take a peek inside," she suggested. She opened her shoulder bag, pulled out her lock-picking kit, and quickly opened the door.

Stan chuckled as he stepped inside behind her. "Nice job, Nancy. Anytime you need a partner, give me a call."

Inside, the house was cool and dark. All the curtains had been drawn, and the windows were shut tight. Nancy glanced into the small living room to the left of the foyer. The only furniture was a gray sofa and one end table. It didn't look as if Leah had planned to stay long.

"I'll start upstairs," Nancy said. She sprinted up the steps by twos, while Stan headed for the kitchen.

"I'll stay here as lookout," Ned volunteered.

Upstairs, Nancy looked for the bedroom that seemed the most lived-in. When she stepped into the largest bedroom, she saw two canvas suitcases on the bed. She quickly unzipped a maroon one and ran her hands through the layers of clothes. Shorts, sandals, sundresses, T-shirts. Definitely clothes for a cruise, Nancy decided.

Suddenly her fingers felt something flat and stiff. Closing her hand around two thin rectangular booklets, she pulled them out. She immediately recognized that they were United States passports.

With trembling fingers, Nancy opened the first one. A picture of Leah O'Halloran stared back at her. Dropping it back into the suitcase, Nancy opened the other passport. Even though the person in the photo had a beard, she easily recognized Nick Lazlo. The name on his passport was Bill Jobeson.

"Bingo," Nancy murmured. "We have our proof."

"Nancy!" She jumped at the sound of Ned's urgent voice. "Leah's car just turned up the drive."

Quickly Nancy zipped up the first suitcase and opened the second one. If she could just find a brochure or map that gave some clue as to Leah and Nick's destination . . .

Nancy was checking a side pocket of the suitcase when she heard the front door open. Leah was in the house already!

Nancy hoped Ned and Stan had had a chance to hide. Still holding Bill's passport, she zipped up the suitcase. Her heart beating rapidly, she stepped into the hall and frantically looked for a place to hide.

From downstairs came the tap-tapping of high

heels as Leah walked across the wooden floor of the foyer. Nancy caught her breath as she heard the first scrape of a shoe on the staircase. Leah was coming upstairs. In a moment she was going to catch Nancy red-handed!

Chapter

Fifteen

The TAPPING grew louder and quicker. Running as silently as she could, Nancy darted for the front bedroom. She flattened herself against the wall, hiding behind the open door. Then, hardly daring to breathe, she listened.

Sharp footsteps tapped rapidly down the hall and into the other bedroom. "Hi, it's me," Nancy heard a woman's voice say. Leah had to be talking on the phone, Nancy guessed. She had seen one on the bedside table.

"Yeah, that nosy chick and the private eye were in the tavern asking Sheila a lot of questions," Leah was saying.

So Leah had been hanging around the tavern. Which meant she could have been there the night Nancy had been knocked into the water.

"You're right, we have to get out of here

now . . . Yeah, fine. Meet you at the marina in an hour."

A few minutes later Nancy heard footsteps in the hall. Leah was going downstairs, Nancy thought. She heard the front door open, close with a loud bang, and then heard it being locked.

Moving from her hiding place, Nancy quickly ran to the front window in the room. Leah was putting the two suitcases into the trunk of her sports car. When Nancy saw her get into the car and start the motor, she hurried downstairs. From the living room window, she could see Leah back the car out of the drive, then turn left and speed off.

Nancy unlocked the front door, then ran onto the porch. Ned was coming around the corner of the house from the back, with Stan right behind him.

"Leah knows we're onto her," Nancy quickly explained. "I heard her tell someone to meet her at the marina in an hour."

"Who's she going to meet?" Stan asked.

Nancy pulled the passport from her purse and held it out to the private investigator. Ned was looking over Stan's shoulder when he opened it, and the two gasped in unison.

"So you were right about Lazlo being alive, Nancy," Ned said, shaking his head in amazement.

"Let's follow Leah to the marina," Stan said. He started across the lawn toward his sedan.

"No!" she blurted out. "If we tip Leah off even more, the two could ditch their current plans and disappear forever."

Stan stopped in his tracks. "You're right." We'd better get to the police instead. After we show them that passport, they're not going to let Mr. Lazlo get very far."

"If they can catch him," Nancy said grimly. "By the time we convince the police, and they notify the Coast Guard, Leah and Nick will have a head start down the Chesapeake Bay."

"So what now?" Ned asked.

Suddenly Nancy had an idea. "Stan, where is Chessie Marina?"

"About two miles south of Annapolis. Why?"

"Andy's meeting us at the City Dock with his sailboat," Nancy explained as she started to jog toward Stan's car. "You can drop Ned and me there and then head to the police station. Do everything in your power to convince them that Nick Lazlo is alive and about to disappear to some tropical island."

"And what have you cooked up for us?" Ned asked Nancy when he caught up with her at the car.

"We're going to follow Leah and Nick."

Ned frowned. "But you just said that would tip them off."

Nancy grinned mischievously. "Not if we're tailing them with another boat!"

* * *

"Nick's alive?" Annabel exclaimed when Nancy and Ned met Andy, Bess, Parker, and Annabel at the City Dock and broke the news to them. Throwing back her head, Annabel burst out laughing. Then abruptly her expression hardened. "That no-good, two-timing jerk. I just hope he's not running off with any of my money!"

When she boarded the sailboat, Nancy glanced over at Andy. He seemed stunned. Parker and Bess were sitting next to him in the cockpit. Parker had his arm around Andy's shoulders, trying to comfort him.

"I can't believe Nick did this to me," Andy said in a low voice. He sounded furious, but Nancy knew that he must be deeply hurt, as well. His childhood friend and partner had stolen money from their business and then set up Andy to take the rap for a murder that had never even happened.

Suddenly Andy jumped up and grabbed the wheel of the *Skipper's Surprise*. "Let's go get him," he said tersely. "I want to be face-to-face with that traitor when I ask him why he did this to me—to *us,*" he corrected himself. His steely gaze settled on Annabel, who was still on the dock. She nodded and without a word started to untie the bowline.

The chase was on.

"Chessie Marina's just around the bend!" Andy shouted half an hour later through the increasing wind.

The *Skipper's Surprise* ripped through the waves of Chesapeake Bay. Thunderheads churned in the darkening sky now, and Nancy could smell approaching rain. The group had donned yellow storm gear and prepared the sailboat for the worst. In the cabin, every loose object had been stowed or secured.

The bad weather might be to their advantage, Nancy reflected as she grabbed for a handhold during a rough pitch. They might be able to tail Leah and Nick without the two knowing.

"So what's the plan?" Annabel called from where she was standing beside Andy at the wheel. "Are we going to try to follow them?"

"Uh, can you drop us off somewhere first?" Bess asked. She and Parker were huddled next to each other in the cockpit. They both looked green.

Nancy reached across the seat and squeezed Bess's hand. Her friend's fingers were ice cold. "Maybe you and Parker should go down into the cabin," Nancy suggested.

Annabel gave Bess and Parker a quick look. "There are some seasickness pills in the medicine chest," she told them. For once, Nancy didn't notice any sarcasm in her voice.

"Good idea," Bess mumbled. She grabbed Parker's hand, and the two stood up. Weaving and swaying with the boat, they clumsily made their way down the ladder and into the galley, then closed the hatch behind them.

"There's the marina!" Andy cried. Nancy could see rows of sailboats and powerboats moored there. "Now what?" Andy asked.

"Now we wait," Nancy told him. Pushing up the sleeve of her slicker, she checked her watch. "If it took Leah an hour to get here, they should have their gear stowed and be ready to sail any minute."

Annabel pointed left toward Chesapeake Bay. "We'll sail in small circles until we see them. We're just north of the marina. They'll be headed south, so they probably won't even look this way."

"And if they do, they won't recognize the *Skipper's Surprise,* anyway," Andy put in. "It's getting too dark. Besides"—he gestured to the stern of the boat—"I've covered up the name with a tarp."

"Good thinking," Nancy said. "When we catch sight of them, we'll radio the Coast Guard and give them the exact location of Nick and Leah's boat. By then Stan and the police should have informed the Coast Guard of what's going on."

Ned jumped into the cockpit from his perch on the deck, where he had just cast off the starboard jib. "The question is, how are we going to recognize the boat Leah and Nick are on?" he asked.

Andy laughed. "They'll be the only ones besides us crazy enough to head out in the middle of a brewing storm."

"Plus, Stan said the marina mentioned the boat they'd bought was a new Sabre Forty," Nancy added. "Do you know what that looks like?" she asked Andy.

"Sure do. In fact, that's one coming out of the marina now." He nodded to his right.

Nancy had already taken out her binoculars. Now she stood up and looked through them. She could see two figures on board, but their faces were hidden under the hoods of their rain gear. On a hunch, Nancy trained the binoculars on the stern. The boat was aptly named *Fooled Them All*.

"That has to be Nick and Leah," she decided. "Andy, are you ready to alert the Coast Guard?"

Andy nodded and went below. Just then the wind hit them from all sides.

"Reef the mainsail!" Annabel shouted above the noise.

Immediately Ned leapt for the boom, where he began to roll up part of the mainsail. Annabel turned the wheel, steering the *Skipper's Surprise* after the Sabre. "Winch in the jib," she directed Nancy. "Then hold on tight. We're going after them!"

"I got the Coast Guard!" Andy announced when he came up the ladder a few minutes later. "Your buddy Stan had them ready and waiting."

Soon after, the rain started to pummel them. Bess and Parker came topside to relieve Ned and Nancy and let them dry off. The *Skipper's Sur-*

prise was still sailing south. Although *Fooled Them All* was racing through the storm, Annabel had managed to keep the other boat's navigational lights in sight. But even after an hour, there was no sign of the Coast Guard.

"Where are they?" Nancy snapped as she paced along the small aisle in the cabin. The sailboat lurched, and she grabbed the edge of the table to keep from falling. "We can't tail them much longer. This storm's getting too nasty."

"Hey, sit down before you fall," Ned said calmly. Grabbing her arm, he guided Nancy next to him in the booth. "We've got to rest up so we can give Annabel and Andy a break."

"You're right. It's just that if Nick makes it to the Atlantic Ocean, we'll lose him—forever."

Ned slipped his arm around Nancy and held her close. "But at least we have the proof to clear Andy." With a chuckle, he said, "Nick Lazlo, alias Bill Jobeson, will be awfully surprised when he finds out that he doesn't have a passport."

"But by then he'll be too far away for us to do anything." Sighing, Nancy laid her head on Ned's shoulder. His hair was damp from the rain, but his arm felt warm and comforting, and Nancy closed her eyes.

A loud scrape announced the opening of the hatch. "We need you guys up here!" Parker yelled.

Without a word, Ned and Nancy scrambled for

their storm gear. When their hoods were fastened, they climbed the ladder to the cockpit.

"What's wrong?" Nancy shouted. Not that she needed to ask. The rain was coming down in sheets. Andy had reefed the mainsail even more, and Parker had taken down the jib. Bess was bailing water from the cockpit, and Annabel's fingers looked as if they were frozen to the wheel.

"We've lost them!" Andy shouted. "I'm going down below to radio their last position to the Coast Guard."

Lost them! The bottom dropped out of Nancy's stomach as a giant wave picked up the boat and dumped it roughly. Grabbing the handrail, Nancy scanned the rough seas in every direction, but it was so dark that she could barely see a few yards beyond the boat.

Her heart sank. In this raging storm, there was no way the Coast Guard would be able to find Nick and Leah's boat. The two were gone forever.

Chapter

Sixteen

I CAN'T BELIEVE we lost them!" Annabel cried out. She looked exhausted as she put her forehead down on the steering wheel.

"I wish this rain would just stop," Bess said in a voice laced with frustration.

As if in answer, the rain suddenly slacked off a little and the wind slowed. Nancy stared at the dark sky.

"I think it's over," Andy said softly, as though he didn't dare believe it was true.

Nancy reached for Annabel's ice-cold hand and gave it a squeeze. "You did great," she told her.

In the next instant, a bright light blinded Nancy.

"What's going on?" Ned asked from on top of

the cabin, where he and Parker had been checking the condition of the mainsail.

"Stay where you are!" a voice commanded through a bullhorn.

Nancy threw up her hands to shield her eyes. Despite the glare, she could make out the shape of a sailboat that had drifted silently up to their starboard side. Its navigational lights had been turned off, and in all the confusion of the storm, no one had noticed it. The floodlight from the other boat made it difficult for her to identify who was speaking on the other boat, but she had a hunch she knew who it was.

Beside her, Annabel sucked in her breath. "Nick Lazlo, you—you—creep!" she shouted furiously.

Someone chuckled from the other boat. By shielding her eyes from the blinding light, Nancy could see the outline of two people standing on the port side of the boat.

"Still so sweet and forgiving, Annabel," Nick Lazlo said sarcastically. "A good sailor, though. I figured I'd lose you hours ago. Too bad you weren't good enough to keep me from circling around behind the *Surprise* during the storm."

"How did you know it was us?" Nancy asked.

Lazlo aimed the light right in Nancy's eyes. "If it isn't Ms. Drew, the big glitch in my whole plan. If you hadn't been so relentless, things never would have come to this."

"Come to what?" Bess asked in a shaky voice.

Lazlo raised a long, slender object in the air, and Nancy shuddered when she realized that it was a rifle.

"Your shipwreck," Nick stated. "Four or five well-placed holes in your hull and the *Skipper's Surprise* will sink like a rock."

"You wouldn't dare!" Annabel screeched. "I'm your wife! Andy is your best friend!"

"Was," Nick corrected. "Andy and his conservative ideas about making an honest buck were getting in my way. And you, dear Annabel, were never much of a wife." Reaching out his arm, he grasped the waist of the woman next to him and pulled her closer. "I think Leah and I are much better suited to each other."

Beside Nancy, Annabel growled low in her throat. Quickly Nancy reached out and put a restraining hand on the woman's arm. Andy was still below radioing the Coast Guard. If he could just get them before Nick Lazlo and Leah got away!

"Don't listen to him, Annabel," Bess whispered. "He's just trying to make you mad."

Nancy cupped her hands around her mouth. She had to do something—anything—to stall Nick. "You wouldn't sink the *Skipper's Surprise,"* she declared. "You worked too hard on this boat."

"And she's the perfect racing boat," Ned

joined in. He caught her gaze, and Nancy realized that he'd picked up on what she was doing.

"That's a laugh." Nick chuckled. "I knew from the first time I sailed her that the keel design was no good. At least, not good enough to make me the fortune Leah and I deserve."

"So you decided to steal money from Lazlo Designs, instead," Parker said from on top of the cabin. Nancy glanced over at him. He was next to Ned, gripping the boom tightly, as if he'd like to use it to knock Lazlo into the water.

"Pretty brilliant, huh," Lazlo replied. "Andy never suspected a thing when I wrote those checks to Steele Lumber on our main account. And all I had to do was intercept the last two bank statements from our special joint account, and he never knew that I'd moved the insurance money into the Steele Lumber account, either. It ended up being quite a nice chunk of money. Enough for Leah and me to live comfortably on some tropical island."

"What about the pirates?" Ned wanted to know.

As Nancy turned to look at her boyfriend, a movement from the bow caught her eye. She could see the forward hatch rising, ever so slowly. Her heart quickened. Andy must be trying to sneak up that way! She had to get Lazlo's attention so he wouldn't notice.

Abruptly she jumped onto the starboard side

of the cockpit. Lazlo swung the light into her eyes.

"Stay where you are," he warned.

"I just wanted to get a closer look at a murderer," Nancy said, pointing at Leah. Through the blinding light, she could see Leah pull away from Nick. "I bet the pirate thing was just a hoax, Mrs. O'Halloran," Nancy went on. "I think that you killed your own husband!"

"And who's going to prove it?" Leah shot back in a cocky voice. "You five are going to be at the bottom of Chesapeake Bay!"

From the corner of her eye, Nancy could see Andy pull himself quietly from the hatch and hunker down on the bow.

Parker must have noticed him, too. Quickly he called over to the other boat. "Why fake your death, Lazlo, then set up my cousin? Why didn't you just split with the money?"

"Because I didn't want to have to run for the rest of my life," Lazlo explained. Nancy could hear the impatience in his voice. She knew they didn't have much longer before he'd blast several holes in the boat. "So I planned to 'die' and come back as Bill Jobeson. I knew Old Bill was going to go any time. All that drinking had ruined his liver. So when he conveniently died Thursday morning, Leah and I put the final part of our plan into action. Setting up Andy was the easy part." He laughed heartily. "Where is that predictable, trusting sucker, anyway? In jail?"

"Arrrgh!" A furious cry came from the bow of the *Skipper's Surprise*. Nancy started in surprise as Andy launched himself into the air across the water, straight toward Lazlo. Nick whirled, but he was too late. Andy knocked him to the deck, and the rifle flew into the air, then clattered onto the roof of the cabin.

"Nick!" Leah screeched. Swinging around, she turned the spotlight away from the *Skipper's Surprise*, focusing it on the two men grappling on the deck.

Nancy quickly judged the distance between the two boats. It was about five feet. Could she make it?

When she saw Leah scrambling for the rifle, Nancy knew she had no choice. She stepped over the lifeline, steadied herself, then jumped. She landed awkwardly on the rail of the other boat. Clutching the lifeline, she pulled herself over. But Leah had reached the rifle. Grabbing the barrel, Leah swung it toward Nancy like a club.

"Oh, no, you don't!" Nancy heard Ned yell. The next thing she knew, a yellow slicker came hurtling through the air. It caught Leah in the face, stopping her just long enough for Nancy to yank the rifle from the woman's grasp and toss it over to Ned. By then Annabel had swung the *Skipper's Surprise* closer to the other boat, and Parker had jumped onto the bow. Together he and Andy subdued Nick. When Ned jumped aboard with the gun and rope, they quickly tied up Nick and Leah.

"Are you guys all right?" Bess shouted from the *Skipper's Surprise*. She had grabbed the lifeline of *Fooled Them All* and temporarily tied the two boats together. Now she joined Annabel at the wheel.

Standing up, Nancy surveyed the group on the bow of *Fooled Them All*. A disgruntled Nick Lazlo and Leah O'Halloran were tied to the mast. Andy, Parker, and Ned were standing over them, with satisfied looks on their faces.

Nancy gave Bess the thumbs-up sign. "Everything's shipshape!"

"So Leah and Nick planned the whole boat theft scheme? Both times?" Andy asked.

It was the next morning, and Nancy, Ned, Bess, Parker, Andy, and Mr. and Mrs. Devereux were sitting on the patio enjoying a sumptuous brunch. Andy's parents had also invited Annabel Lazlo and Stan Yadlowski, to thank them for all their help in clearing Andy.

With a nod, Nancy picked up a sugar-coated strawberry. "Mike O'Halloran was in on the first scam, too. Then Leah must have fallen for Nick and decided that three was a crowd."

"My sources at the police department say that Nick and Leah are both singing like birds," Stan spoke up. "Leah's blaming everything on Nick, and he's blaming everything on her."

Annabel gave a disgusted snort. "At least I know Nick's a selfish jerk with all women." Nancy noticed that Annabel had hardly touched her food and there were dark circles under her amber eyes. Nancy couldn't help feeling sorry for the woman. Even though her marriage hadn't been a happy one, it had to be painful to find out that her husband was an even worse scoundrel than she had suspected.

"I still don't understand why Nick sabotaged his own boats," Andy's father said. He and Mrs. Devereux were sitting across from Andy. "They'd already been sold. Lazlo Designs would have made a lot of money from the sale."

"Which Nick would have had to split with Andy," Nancy said. "Nick was too greedy for that. Besides, he didn't sabotage the boats. From what the police told us, Leah and Mike contacted him a while ago saying that they knew of foreign customers who wanted to buy boats 'under the table.'"

"I get it," Ned cut in. "Nick sold the boats to the foreign customers, then had Leah and Mike deliver them. They'd rendezvous in the middle of the ocean. Then to collect *again* from the insurance company, they concocted the story about the first boat sinking and pirates stealing the second boat."

"I bet Leah and Nick have the money from the sale to the foreigners deposited in a secret account in another country," Nancy said.

Andy was shaking his head. "I've got to hand it to Nick, it was a brilliant plan. Even when the insurance company started getting suspicious, he had it covered. Plan his own death and set me up for it."

Giving Andy a knowing look, Annabel said, "I told you Nick was a snake, but you're so trusting! You probably even gave him a copy of the key to the drawer where you kept your gun."

"Uh, as a matter of fact, I did," Andy admitted, his cheeks reddening. "But Nick was my friend! I never would've guessed that he'd turn on me . . ." His voice trailed off, and he stared down at his plate.

"He planned his so-called disappearance well in advance," Nancy said to Andy. "That's why you never guessed what was going on."

"Plus, he was very smart," Ned added. "After that argument at the party, he had us all believing someone was out to get him. I bet the person he was 'fighting' with was Leah, pretending to be the irate competitor."

"So Nick must have rigged the mast, too," Bess put in, "figuring that everybody would guess that it was meant to fall on him."

Parker sighed. "He never even let on that the keel design was a sham."

"That's for sure," Andy said glumly. "My boatbuilding friend confirmed that. And that means that Lazlo Designs is about to go down the tubes." He sighed. "I don't see how I can save the company—we owe too much money from developing the Nican. And even if the insurance money *is* recovered, it would just go back to Bayside Insurance, since the claim was fraudulent. The most I could ever collect is the money Nick took from our main account. And fifteen thousand won't go very far."

Andy's mother reached over to pat his shoulder. "At least you're not in jail," she said comfortingly.

"If it's any consolation, Nick told the police that he was going to send proof that you didn't kill him," Stan said as he bit into another muffin.

"Oh, that was sweet of him," Annabel said. "I just bet he was going to write a cutesy letter from some faraway island where he was living on all of Andy's money." Then she shrugged. "But at least he didn't get *my* money. And now that he's bound for a long jail sentence, I can happily divorce him."

Nancy looked at Andy. She had expected to see him brighten at the news, but he didn't react. "Don't look so gloomy, Andy," Nancy told him. "Maybe there's still a way you can save Lazlo Designs."

"I doubt it," Andy said. "I'll have to sell the company to pay all the debts from developing the Nican."

Suddenly Annabel sat bolt upright in her chair.

"What is all this pessimistic talk? And why would you even think about selling the company, Andrew Devereux?"

Everyone stopped eating to stare at Annabel.

"I'll be your new partner," Annabel went on. "After all, I've got plenty of money *and* sailing experience." Standing up, she opened her arms wide. "So what if the keel design is a little off. We'll design a new one, a *better* one."

Andy was staring at Annabel, a glimmer of hope in his eyes. "Are you serious?"

Annabel snorted. "Of course I'm serious. On one condition. That the new line of boats isn't called the Nican Forty."

"Why don't you name it the Anna Forty," Bess suggested.

Annabel looked around the table, grinning at each person in turn. "Hey, I like that!"

Everyone broke out laughing. Standing up, Andy raised his glass of orange juice in the air. "Let's toast the new Anna Forty." He turned toward Nancy, who was leaning against Ned, his arm around her shoulder. "And to Nancy Drew, who solved this crazy case *and* who also learned how to grind that jib like the best of sailors!"

Nancy's next case:

Nancy's in Sarasota, Florida, winter site of the Grand Royal Circus, to help trapeze artist Natalia Petronov look into her heritage. Adopted as an infant, Natalia is now determined to find her real father. But as Nancy searches for clues in a shadowy past, one thing becomes instantly clear in the present: Natalia's life is at risk!

Natalia flies through the air with the greatest of ease—until someone messes with her trapeze. And whoever's playing tricks is definitely *not* clowning around. The circus of danger is about to begin, and in the center ring lies a deadly secret. The search for the truth could lead Natalia—or Nancy—to take a hard fall . . . without a net . . . in *DANGEROUS RELATIONS*, Case #82 in the Nancy Drew Files™.

Most Archway Paperbacks are available at special quantity discounts for bulk purchases for sales promotions, premiums or fund raising. Special books or book excerpts can also be created to fit specific needs.

For details write the office of the Vice President of Special Markets, Pocket Books, 1230 Avenue of the Americas, New York, New York 10020.

NANCY DREW® AND
THE HARDY BOYS®
TEAM UP FOR MORE MYSTERY...
MORE THRILLS...AND MORE
EXCITEMENT THAN EVER BEFORE!

A NANCY DREW AND HARDY BOYS
SUPERMYSTERY
by Carolyn Keene

In the NANCY DREW AND HARDY BOYS SuperMystery, Nancy's unique sleuthing and Frank and Joe's hi-tech action-packed approach make for a dynamic combination you won't to miss!

☐ DOUBLE CROSSING   74616-2/$3.99
☐ A CRIME FOR CHRISTMAS   74617-0/$3.50
☐ SHOCK WAVES   74393-7/$3.99
☐ DANGEROUS GAMES   74108-X/$3.50
☐ THE LAST RESORT   67461-7/$3.99
☐ THE PARIS CONNECTION   74675-8/$3.99
☐ BURIED IN TIME   67463-3/$3.99
☐ MYSTERY TRAIN   67464-1/$3.99
☐ BEST OF ENEMIES   67465-X/$3.99
☐ HIGH SURVIVAL   67466-8/$3.50
☐ NEW YEAR'S EVIL   67467-6/$3.99
☐ TOUR OF DANGER   67468-4/$3.99
☐ SPIES AND LIES   73125-4/$3.99
☐ TROPIC OF FEAR   73126-2/$3.99

Simon & Schuster Mail Order
200 Old Tappan Rd., Old Tappan, N.J. 07675

Please send me the books I have checked above. I am enclosing $_____ (please add $0.75 to cover the postage and handling for each order. Please add appropriate sales tax). Send check or money order–no cash or C.O.D.'s please. Allow up to six weeks for delivery. For purchase over $10.00 you may use VISA: card number, expiration date and customer signature must be included.

Name _____

Address _____

City _____ State/Zip _____

VISA Card # _____ Exp.Date _____

Signature _____
                                                        664